Dear Preston,

I was a survivor when you were here, and I'm a survivor now that you're gone, though it isn't as easy. Sometimes I think you hated that about me, that things looked so easy for me, but I take the laid-back position because it's the one that gives me the best advantage. And I ain't goin' out like you, bro. I've seen some butt-ugly phenomena in the past two years, starting with you squeezing the trigger, but I'll be damned if I'll take your road.

ALSO BY CHRIS CRUTCHER

KING OF THE MILD FRONTIER: *An Ill-Advised Autobiography*

RUNNING LOOSE

STOTAN!

THE CRAZY HORSE ELECTRIC GAME

ATHLETIC SHORTS: *Six Short Stories*

STAYING FAT FOR SARAH BYRNES

IRONMAN

WHALE TALK

CHRIS CRUTCHER

CHINESE HANDCUFFS

A Greenwillow Book

HarperTempest

An Imprint of HarperCollins*Publishers*

For Tracy and Paige

Grateful acknowledgment is made for permission
to reprint an excerpt from *Horton Hatches the Egg*,
by Dr. Seuss. Copyright © 1940 and renewed in 1968
by Dr. Seuss. By permission of Random House, Inc.

Library of Congress Cataloging-in-Publication Data
Crutcher, Chris.
    Chinese handcuffs / by Chris Crutcher.
        p.   cm.
    "Greenwillow Books."
    Summary: Still troubled by his older brother's violent suicide,
eighteen-year-old Dillon becomes deeply involved in the terrible
secret of his friend Jennifer, who feels she can tell no one what
her stepfather is doing to her.
    ISBN 0-688-08345-5 — ISBN 0-06-059839-5 (pbk.)
    [1. Child abuse—Fiction. 2. Suicide—Fiction. 3. Brothers—
Fiction.] I. Title.
PZ7.C89Ch 1989   88-45809
[Fic]—dc19   CIP
                                                              AC

Typography by R. Hult
15 16 17 18 OPM 20 19 18 17 16 15 14 13 12 11
❖
First HarperTempest edition, 2004
Visit us on the World Wide Web!
www.harperteen.com

PROLOGUE

A hundred yards from shore, Dillon Hemingway switches to breaststroke, pulling hard with his arms, while letting his legs follow in an easy whip kick, readying them for the transition into the fifty-mile bike ride. At sixteen—a high school junior—this is his second triathlon, and he's learned well from the first, learned to take his advantage over most others in the water, but not to burn himself out there—there's too far left to go.

He tears off his goggles and hands them to Stacy, poised with his bicycle and his gym shorts, which he pulls on over the wet suit as she hands him his Reeboks. The socks are a little hard to get on over his wet feet, and he loses some time drying them; but all in all, the transition isn't bad, considering he hasn't spent the money for the correct cross-training gear. In a very few seconds he is on the bike and gathering speed.

At twenty-five miles, shooting through the regional park, a number of the better bikers have passed him, but he's holding his own, still leading in the fifteen to nineteen age-group. At forty miles a woman with a small child in a bike seat passes him on a steep hill, and he makes a mental note to work harder on the bike leg of the competition. The child smiles and waves, and Dillon starts to laugh—nearly hard enough to bring him to a stop.

He's off the bike at the switch point, and Stacy slaps his butt as she hands him a bottle of Gatorade and a piece of welcome advice. "Get your butt in gear," she says, and he tries to smile but only drools and takes off down the road for the 13.2-mile half-marathon that will take him to the finish line in the middle of Riverfront Park.

As in his initial triathlon, his knees nearly buckle at the onset of the long downhill grade that makes up the first two miles of the race, and he remembers—too late—he was supposed to gear down the bike in the last couple of miles to allow for the transition. He is three miles into the run before his knees finally lose their consistency of warm rubber and he is able to fall into his pace. Drawing from a novel he read recently, called *Dog*

Soldiers, he envisions a perfect triangle in the back of his skull, then scans his body for pain, visually placing it within the borders of the triangle to make it tolerable. He puts the memory of his brother in there, too, but the triangle will not hold him.

Ten miles into the run he begins to fade, despite taking nourishment at all the aid stations and cutting his pace back. At twelve miles the borders of the triangle begin to deteriorate and the burning pain commences to leak out all over him. Anguish fills the spaces between his muscle strands, and his calves threaten to make fists and drive him to the ground. He keeps them stretched, pulling his toes back toward the leg and striking the ground heel first. The idea of trying to catch anyone ahead of him floats away, and he concentrates only on holding off those coming. A bald man, easily forty-five, shoots by, followed by a woman in her twenties. He picks up his pace and stays with the woman for about a hundred yards before she kicks in and leaves him dazzled. Dillon stumbles across the finish line and falls to the side of the path, onto the cool grass, where he lies there on his back, in immense pain, laughing and forcing his toes back toward his shins to hold off the dancing cramp muscles in his legs.

"Keep walking," an official says kindly. "Keep

walking or we'll need a rack to stretch your legs out."

Dillon nods, trying to rise, but the cramps bring him to the ground. He laughs to keep from crying and says, "Shoot me," to the official. "Please. Shoot me."

The official smiles and walks away.

"Not to end the pain," Dillon yells after him. "To end the stupidity."

Thirty minutes later, when his calf muscles have stopped their samba and he can walk around without being tackled from within, Dillon finds himself face-to-face with a local TV newsman informing him he has won his age-group and asking for an interview.

"Sure," Dillon says, running his hand through his hair in a dismal attempt at rapid grooming. Streaks of white follow the lines of his muscular body, the salty residue of a flood of liquids coursing through him over the past four hours.

"I don't usually do sports," the reporter says. "I'm substituting today. Help me out with the terms if I need it, okay?" He guides Dillon to a spot on the grass before a huge pine tree and introduces himself as Wayne Wisnett, a fact Dillon already knows from watching the evening news on Channel 6.

When the camera rolls, Wayne asks a few questions

about what it was like out there, to which Dillon's answers amount to "Hard."

When the newscaster discovers Dillon is but a junior at Chief Joseph High School, he marvels at his size and makes the guess, on the air, that Dillon must be *some kind* of prep school athlete.

"Nope," Dillon says. "This is all I do. I want to qualify for the Ironman someday. It's in Hawaii. And it's exactly twice this far."

"Your football and track coaches must be banging their heads against the locker doors," Wayne Wisnett says into the camera.

"I wouldn't be surprised," Dillon says, smiling. "Could I just say one thing?"

"Sure," the newscaster says. "I'd say you've earned it."

Dillon looks squarely into the camera and breaks into an enormous toothy grin. "I'd just like to thank Mr. John Caldwell, the principal at my school, for making all this possible."

CHAPTER 1

Dear Preston,

Gotta tell you this feels weird. I got the idea from a book called *The Color Purple*, by a lady named Alice Walker. It's a good book—a *really* good book—but that's not the point. The main character didn't have anyone in the real world to talk to, no one she could trust, so she started writing letters to God, because It (that's the pronoun she used for God because she wasn't all that sure of His or Her gender) was about the only thing left she believed in. Since you've been gone, I've been running around so full of that day and everything that probably led up to it that if I don't tell somebody about it, I might just explode. Only there's no one to tell. I can't burden Dad with it; he certainly has enough other things to worry about, what with Mom and Christy having left and working his ass off like he's always done. And Stacy's got her own stuff to deal with about you. Anyway, as you probably know, I have a pretty splotchy history with God, so that leaves you. And why not? You're about the only thing I can think of that *I* believe in. I mean, man, you are *real* to me now. I can let down with you now because I know I won't have to take any shit back like I did all the time when you were alive.

When people ask, I tell them that you escaped back into the universe by your own hand. Pretty poetic characterization for blasting your brains out, don't you think? Hey, I always was a man of letters. I've decided I want to be a writer someday, and Coach says (she's still the best teacher I ever had) that to pull that off, I have to *write*. That is the ulterior motive for writing you, considering the chances of your actually ever reading any of this.

I think everyone thought I'd come back to school after your funeral all quiet and humble and keep my smart mouth shut and just graduate. People treat death funny, like they think after someone's had a close brush with it, all the humor is supposed to go out of their lives and they're supposed to get real serious about things. That's not what happened to me, though. In some ways I felt even more alive after you were gone, and whatever it is in me that doesn't like to get pushed around or take things for granted just because adults say them got bigger.

Anyway, at the end of this year, when I graduate summa

cum desperate from this jive time educational wasteland, there'll be some major backslapping and cap throwing by Mr. Caldwell and some faculty members, who—looking back—would just as soon have seen me graduate the same day I walked in. Caldwell is the vice-principal in charge of discipline now—worked his way up from coach, through counselor, and he claims his position was created the day you and I enrolled. Man's got no better manners than to speak ill of the dead. It's flattering, but I know it's not true. I haven't had it any tougher academically than I ever had—hell, since I've been here, I've pulled down more As than an aardvark in an Appalachian avalanche—it's just that they've had to spend so many would-be educational man-hours trying to keep me under control. I have to say I sympathize to some extent; I have a pretty hard time keeping myself under control sometimes. But boy, they haven't made it easy. I might say that your having preceded me by two years as a drug-crazed biker hasn't exactly made my road any easier. But that was your choice.

I haven't turned into a jerk or anything, at least not by my standards, but it's been real hard getting the powers around here—especially Caldwell—to understand my *meaning*, which has become important to me. There isn't much time. You taught me that. He's been so busy finding different ways to tell me what is and isn't good for me he never *hears* me. The message is pretty simple actually: Everything I am doing *isn't* good for me and everything I'm not doing *is*. Caldwell could certainly have saved a lot of energy by saying it only once. Hell, I've always heard him; I just never agreed.

"Comedy is tragedy standing on its head with its pants down." Remember that? Somebody famous said it first, but I think you and I heard it from Dad, back when I was too young to know what it meant. I know what it means now, though, because I gotta say, Preston, I've seen about enough tragedy in my life to last me the rest of it, and sometimes when I can't find the humor anywhere, well, that's when I get pretty close to the edge. I guess that's where you were.

I got your note. Real creative. "That time with the cat. Don't ever forget." You really went out of your way with the details. I guess you were talking about Charlie, right? I got it. When I showed the note to Dad, I didn't tell all, only "It's just about this cat we killed when we were little." I couldn't stand for him to know more. I tell you, Preston, even eight years after the fact, Charlie's memory still brings me to my knees. I've never been able to write him off as merely the victim of a vicious, senseless childhood prank. I guess you couldn't either.

When I think back on it, losing your legs on the Harley was almost worse than when you finally killed yourself, at least for me. You were never really the same after that, no matter how hard you tried. It was hard to talk about that; you always just cut me off. That was the first time I knew how much I liked it that so many people thought we were twins—when we weren't anymore. I really missed that. I used to pretend we were, you know, even though you were two years older. I never thought about how hard that must have been for you, me being so big and you so little. I just figured Stacy was our great equalizer. No matter how good I was at sports or music or humor or *anything*, she loved you. There were times I would have traded all my size and talent to have her. God, I *hated* that she loved you.

You know, when you think about it, Mom and Dad must have had a pretty goddamn shallow gene pool. Remember how old Phil Roberts down at the Pastime Tavern used to say it looked like you were born on one day, then turned around and spit me out on the next? I don't think we were so close we could have switched partners on a double date, or shown up for each other's detention, but often as not, folks had to take a quick second look to see which one of us had just gone by.

I guess that's about as far as the resemblance went, though, right? I mean, you were one focused dude, at least before you started in on drugs. I always thought if I looked in the dictionary under *intense*, your picture would be there instead of a definition. I think your sense of humor hit the road about three days before you were born—no offense. That didn't leave you with much for the hard times, nothing to help spring yourself back with when life hammered you flat, which seemed often. I mean, from the moment he walked into John R. Rogers Kindergarten, Preston Hemingway took shit from *no* one. They used to stand in line to give you shit. I think I could count on one partially amputated hand the times I saw you laugh out loud.

But me, I was a survivor when you were here, and I'm a survivor now that you're gone, though it isn't as easy. Sometimes I think you hated that about me, that things looked so easy for me, but I take the laid-back position because it's the one that gives me the best advantage. And I ain't goin' out like you, bro. I've seen some butt-ugly phenomena in the past two years, starting with you squeezing the trigger, but I'll be damned if I'll take your road. Might as well be straight about it. I loved you and should *anyone* speak ill of your name, I'll mop the place up with him; but you left by the back door and you left early, and to my way of thinking that's a cowardly way out. Dillon Hemingway is going to by God be here when the smoke clears. And if there's any way, he'll be here laughing.

11

Well, that's probably enough for now. Actually, I like this. Maybe it'll work. You'll be hearing from me.

Your brother,
Dillon

Ten-year-old Preston Hemingway stands at the rear of an eight-month-old Saint Bernard, slapping him lightly in the face with his own tail, challenging him to a duel. His eight-year-old brother, Dillon, leans against the side of the garage, laughing, cheering for the dog. The dog is named Blitz, short for Blitzkrieg, a favorite word their father, a Vietnam vet and amateur historian, uses to describe how the Germans fought World War II.

Blitz takes a couple of trial bites at the furry sword in Preston's hands, then charges after it like a beast gone haywire as Preston jumps back. Blitz chomps down and holds on, spinning faster and faster, Preston loudly urging him to stay with it for eight seconds if he wants the points. The giant dog stops suddenly, his tail sandwiched between immense jaws, like an embarrassed teddy bear, staring at Dillon rolling on the ground with glee. He senses the joke is on him and releases his hold. The tail falls free.

"Again! Again!" Dillon chants, and Preston reaches

again for the tail; but Blitz has had enough and bolts from his grasp, woofing twice loudly, before lumbering across the back alley into Mrs. Crummet's yard. Both boys holler at him to get back in this yard right this minute; but that only serves to make him run faster, and before he knows it, he's face-to-face with Charlie the Cat.

It's a known fact that if there's an animal in all of Three Forks meaner than Mrs. Crummet, it's Mrs. Crummet's cat, a three-legged alley tom with a face like a dried-up creek bed and the temperament of a freeway sniper. *Mean* cats call Charlie mean. He chewed that other leg off extracting himself from a muskrat trap, and he's utterly willing to let anyone, man or beast, know that experience left him feelin' right poorly toward the world and every living thing in it.

Before the boys can act, a high-pitched screech cuts through the neighborhood, followed by the frantic song of a panicky half-grown St. Bernard. Blitz streaks back into the yard, bleeding profusely from a two-inch slice across his nose. Mrs. Crummet is at the edge of her yard, cackling and shaking her bony finger at Preston and Dillon as if they were Hansel and Gretel. "You boys keep that mangy dog out of my yard or Charlie'll have him for breakfast. Do you hear me? Do you *hear* me?"

"Shut up, you old bag," Preston yells back. "Our

dog didn't do anything to your stupid cat. Or your yard either."

"You watch your filthy mouth, young man. I have a mind to tell your momma what you just said."

"Go ahead," Preston shouts back. "My momma thinks you're an old bag, too."

Mrs. Crummet starts to speak, her skinny finger aimed at Preston like a poison dart gun, but she has nothing to say. Everybody thinks she's an old bag. *She* thinks she's an old bag.

She whirls and stomps toward her door. At the porch she whirls again, eyes blazing, voice vibrating with tension. "If that dog comes back in my yard," she says, "I'll call the police."

The chief of police in Three Forks is Finas Hemingway, Caulder Hemingway's brother, Dillon and Preston's uncle.

In early evening, just after dinner, Preston and Dillon let themselves out the back door and through the clear, balmy evening toward the garage, Preston carrying a gunnysack and Dillon a paper bag full of leftovers from supper. While Preston seals off the hole leading to the adjoining woodshed and a three-inch space between the overhead doors and the garage floor, Dillon spreads a trail of food from the edge of Mrs. Crummet's backyard to the side door, which they leave slightly ajar. Then they sit behind it in the dark, munching a package of chocolate-covered graham crackers, and wait. Soon enough, following his stomach to the heart of their trap, comes Charlie. He stops at the crack in the door, and for a moment Dillon thinks—maybe wishes—he's going to turn around and go home, but Charlie creeps silently inside. A loud crack breaks the silence as Preston kicks the door shut. Dillon's heart beats like a jackhammer as the guttural growl spilling out of Charlie says he knows there's danger. Preston flips on a flashlight, shining it directly into Charlie's eyes, and Charlie freezes, crouched, eyes blazing red. In an instant the gunnysack is over him and Preston wraps him up.

"Now, you son of a bitch," Preston says, "we'll teach you to mess with our dog."

Dillon says, "Yeah, you son of a bitch."

Charlie squirms and fights in the sack like two badgers soaked in hot tar, his voice shrill and powerful, filled with terror and rage. Preston flips the switch to the dim overhead light and slowly begins swinging the sack in a circle above his head, then faster and faster as Charlie's wails bounce off the thin plyboard walls. In a flash he slings the sack at the old wood stove in the corner, scoring a direct hit on the door handle, and the room is filled with the sickening thud. Dillon is frozen to his spot, filled with horror and tremendous excitement, and Preston leaps for the sack just as Charlie's head appears in the opening. He stuffs the cat back inside; but Charlie gets a piece of his hand with his front claw, and Preston swears.

"Okay, you son of a bitch," he says between gritted teeth, nostrils flaring, "if that's the way you want it . . ." He steps back and again flings Charlie hard against the stove.

Dillon says, "Yeah, you son of a bitch. We'll teach you now."

Charlie's pitch changes. He knows, at some level where all living things know, that he's going to die, and he's scratching and clawing and screeching to the end. Preston hoists the sack, beats it endlessly against the floor, then loses his grip for an instant. Charlie struggles free. He crawls across the floor toward the door— toward Dillon—and Preston screams, "Get him! Get him! Kill that son of a bitch!"

And Dillon knows it's all way, way too far. He looks into Preston's eyes and sees no one there—and Dillon himself is on the edge. The cat is a mangled, bloody mess, his timbre nearly human. Dillon is frozen, can barely breathe past the huge knot in the back of his throat.

"Get him!" Preston screams again, and now Dillon actually looks to Charlie for help, knowing he can't leave him alive like this and he can't kill him, hoping he'll take pity on them and just roll over. Preston clutches the sack, but Charlie has regained a bit of mobility and struggles more quickly toward the corner. Preston tosses Dillon a tire iron from the workbench as he moves to cut the cat off. "I'll scare him back," he whispers, "and you let him have it." He slaps the sack on the floor, and Charlie turns back toward Dillon, low, like a cornered serpent, and in a blinding instant Dillon brings the tire iron down on his head. Charlie squirms, then flops, his one hind leg jerking involuntarily. Dillon is in it now, all the way. He brings the tire iron down again, then again, until Charlie is still. Electric adrenaline burns through Dillon, and he proceeds to beat Charlie's still body until Preston seizes his wrist in mid-swing. "That's it," he says. "We got him." He breathes deeply. "That'll teach him to mess with our dog."

"Yeah," Dillon says. "That'll teach him." But in that moment he knows something is terribly wrong, and Preston knows it, too. Neither speaks, but they stand gazing down at Charlie for an eternity in the dim light of the suddenly forsaken garage, wanting to go back—to step back over that treacherous, mysterious sliver of time that brought them here—and make it different.

The boys bury Charlie in the dirt next to the alley, up against the garage, bury him deep, so deep no one will ever find him. Dillon has their grandfather's old World War II folding blade army shovel, and he just can't stop digging. He wants to dig so deep that if anyone finds Charlie, it will be someone Chinese; but Preston finally stops him, and they throw Charlie's mutilated body into the hole and cover him up. They can't throw the dirt over him fast enough, and when Charlie's covered, Dillon places a crate filled with rusty car engine parts over the loose dirt, not so much to hide the evidence as to make sure Charlie stays put.

Inside, Annie Hemingway offers them dessert, and they accept it in order to appear as if things were normal, and they sit on the couch, eating and watching a rerun of "Star Trek." Caulder Hemingway says to judge from all the commotion out there, some hot little feline number must be roaming the neighborhood; that she'd best stay out of Charlie's yard if she doesn't want catdom's ugliest babies. Caulder has always said Charlie was probably the last living thing to crawl out of the La Brea tar pits.

But Dillon is thinking now, maybe he wasn't all that ugly, and he doesn't want to hear any jokes about

Charlie, and neither does Preston. So Dillon pretends to fall asleep toward the end of "Star Trek," then jumps up and runs to bed.

Sometime later, way after midnight, with his heart hammering its way through his breastbone and his head movies running amok, Dillon throws back the covers and sneaks across the upstairs hall to Preston's room. Preston's door stands open, and light from a nearly full moon washes in through his six-pane windows, casting shadowy crosses across the foot of his bed and onto the floor. Dillon slips in carefully and makes his way to the edge of his bed, where he sits.

"Can't sleep either, huh?" Preston says into the darkness.

"Nope."

Preston says, "Yeah."

Dillon is quiet a moment, then: "Preston, you think there's something wrong with us?"

Preston takes a deep breath, lets it out slowly, but doesn't answer.

"Preston?"

"I don't know, Dillon. Maybe there is." His voice is choked and Dillon knows he's crying.

As the tears well up from deep inside, Dillon sees the spillway gate up at the earth dam rising—water from the reservoir rushing under with unstoppable force. There is no sound, only wave after wave of tears in silent convulsions. "We have to tell," he says when he can finally talk, but Preston's head shakes rapidly— more a vibration, really.

"No," he says. "We can't ever tell anyone. Ever."

In the dim bluish moonglow of the dead of night the boys make a solemn pact never, ever to tell.

P.S. It's later and I've been thinking about Charlie. I don't know much about Christianity, barely enough to blaspheme. But on the basis of what I do know, I think I accept Charlie the Cat as a major Saint; he's the one who taught me not to judge. Since the day he died, I can't look at the horror in *anyone* without looking at the horror in myself.

I know we promised not to tell about Charlie, Pres, but I did. I told Stacy—years later, when the gentle cushion of time and space allowed me to venture a closer look and after you were dead—and she said it was a *leak*, a wrinkle where the coordinates of our individual time and circumstance come together at an odd angle and a crack appears in the structure we've built to keep ourselves decent, and our own personal evil seeps out. Leave it to Stacy to put it in language that would send William Buckley scrambling for his thesaurus, huh? It's one of the hard ways, she says, that we learn human beings are connected by the ghastly as well as the glorious, and we need always to walk around inside ourselves looking for those leaks. And plugging them up. In the end, maybe that's where you failed.

You know, Preston, if you hadn't gone off into that shadowy, savage drug world and come back all beaten up and broken in your heart, if you hadn't finally wanted out, I might have been a little easier to handle by Caldwell and anyone else who thought he ought to be handling me; but I have this whole new sense of urgency now, and I can get downright nasty when someone tries to slow me down, especially when it's some unconscious nosewipe with an idea where my life should be headed and how long it ought to take me to get there.

But maybe not; maybe there is no handling me. Your memory isn't the only thing that fuses me to my passions. Stacy does—even though she's still yours—in some ways. Jen in others. I don't think you know who she is.

To tell the truth, I'm not doing any better with the American concept of boys and girls coming of age than I ever was. Certainly that has some to do with my being willing to crawl across ten miles of crushed glass in my Bermuda shorts to hear Stacy belch into a tin can over the telephone when it was *you* she liked, but even apart from that, it's difficult for me to fathom why they tell you you can have only one member of the opposite sex in your life at one time. In fact, I don't even know who "they" is, so it's hard for me to know even if that's reliable information, but it seems to be *accepted* information. I've tried to accept it. But for me there's Stacy and Jen. Stacy's big in my past—if mostly in my past *dreams*—and Jen seems big in my present, which would be great except that my past runs right into my present and in some ways—most ways—right on into my future. Add to that confusion the fact that I can't tell the difference between being horny and being in love and you might begin to envision the width and depth of my dilemma.

Sometimes I feel I'm inside Jen's head. God, I wish you knew her, Pres. From the day I first saw her at Chief Joe, the first day of our junior year, I was drawn to her like a masochist to hot tongs. Up lit my eyes, and over to her I went. It wasn't lust or lechery or any of the baser passions that usually get me sauntering toward some girl's locker between classes, digging into my bullshit bag of emotional magnets for the one that will pull her tight. What drew me to Jen was that magical sense of connection that goes beyond time and experience together, that sense that we already shared important knowledge—even if that knowledge was dark. It doesn't happen often, but when it does, it's powerful stuff. Screwballs like Stacy, no offense, would tell you Jen and I probably knew each other in another life, but unless Stace wants to offer me a close encounter of the physical kind, she'll be hard pressed to get me believing anyone who had spent one life here would re-up for a second.

Anyway, those two ladies are in my life right now, and though they're as different from each other as either is from me—and neither wants into my pants—they give me what I need, and I wouldn't be with one to the exclusion of the other, though Stacy's been gone a lot and that hasn't been tested. I don't believe in ownership, and luckily for me, neither do they.

You can't talk about Jen without talking about hoops, just as you can't talk about Stacy—at least *I* can't—without talking about you. Jen is probably the best athlete at her sport, male or female, at Chief Joe, and that's coming from *me*, easily the best male athlete, as you no doubt heard me say from time to time. It might be hard to get consensus from the athletic department, because I still don't play any sports here, though every coach in every sport except golf and tennis has tried to recruit me. I don't want to brag, but you should see me now, Pres. I think I could make varsity for any one of them. I just haven't found anyone I wanted to play for. Like I said, I'm still hard to control.

Actually part of what I just wrote is a lie: I *do* like to brag. That's not new to you.

CHAPTER 2

Generally speaking, driving into Jennifer Lawless's territory was like water skiing in shark-infested waters behind a slow boat. Sooner or later you'd lose your ass. Practice was no different from a game to Jennifer, and today was no exception. The first team worked a zone defense, and she owned every inch of hardwood invisibly marked off to be hers. Three times Sandra Madison, the sinewy whippet of a second-string point guard, had tried to drive on her, and three times Jennifer's lightning-quick hands whipped in like a snake's tongue and batted the ball away, once into the bleachers and twice into her own teammates' hands. On Sandy's fourth try, Jennifer feigned fatigue (Sandy should have known better), let Sandy smell the path to the hoop, then moved in a flash to an intersecting point and took the charge, hands in the air, crashing butt first to the floor.

"That's our ball," Jennifer said, smiling, then waved a friendly index finger side to side in front of Sandy's nose. "Don't come in here."

Sandy picked up the ball and checked her body parts. "Don't worry."

The whistle blew, signaling the onset of conditioning drills, and as the girls lined up, Coach Sherman motioned to Jennifer, who approached like a racehorse following a tough workout, shoulder-length blond hair clinging to her neck like a wet mane, her long, sinewy legs glistening with sweat. Standing face-to-face, the two looked like images through a twenty-year mirror, identical long, strong bodies nearing six feet in height, identical hair color, even the same intense eyes.

"Hey, Jen," her coach said with a laugh, "save a little of that for Wenatchee, okay? I want you in one piece."

"I'm okay," Jennifer said. "Sandy didn't hurt me. I mean, look at her. . . ."

"It hurts *me*," Coach said. "When your body hits the floor like that, it rattles my skeleton. Indulge an old lady, okay? I have to be ready for Wenatchee, too."

Jennifer smiled and slapped the coach on the butt as

she headed for the baseline where the rest of the players lined up for sprints. "Okay, Coach," she hollered back over her shoulder. "I'll take it easy. From here to Saturday it's strictly powder puff."

Kathy Sherman turned and walked back toward the bench while Rich Shively, her assistant, ran the girls through their postpractice sprints. Scott Wakefield from the *Three Forks Free Press* waited patiently to get a few comments about the upcoming Wenatchee game.

"What'sa matter, Scotty? Boys' teams all have the night off?"

Wakefield laughed, well aware of Coach Sherman's running contention that girls' athletics took a backseat to boys' down at his paper. The *Free Press* had printed her thoughts on that very subject several times. He had even defended his paper in a local TV debate with her earlier in the year, saying it covered what the people wanted to know. "So does the *Enquirer*," Kathy had shot back.

"You guys are what's hot," Wakefield said now. "If this game with Wenatchee lives up to half the hype, you won't have to worry about female obscurity in athletics for a long time. I'd suggest you don't lose this one, dearie. You're tomorrow's lead on the prep school page."

"Then I think I'll tape what we say," Coach said teasingly. "And if you quote one wrong word, you'll hear about it on all three TV newscasts tomorrow night. *Dearie.*"

"Jeez," Wakefield said in mock defense, "I should get a tape recorder myself."

"All the big boys have 'em," Kathy said. "Considering your note-taking history—with me at least—it might be money well spent."

"So," Wakefield started, pulling his trusty notebook from his shirt pocket, "I'd like to come at this from the Lawless-Halfmoon angle."

"You and every two-bit yellow journalist in the state," Kathy said. "This is a *team* sport, Scotty. You know I don't use the star system."

"I ought to know that, for as many times as you've told me, Coach. But you have to admit there haven't been two athletes of this caliber going head-to-head for quite a while. And for all the complaining you do about chicks not getting any ink, you don't help much when you protect them the way you do."

"So what do you want to know?"

"I want to know how you think Jennifer Lawless is going to stack up against Renee Halfmoon."

"Well," the coach said thoughtfully, "I can't tell you

about Renee Halfmoon, but I can tell you about Jennifer Lawless. She's the most talented athlete I've ever coached if you talk about a balance between raw ability and 'want-to.' I've never met a kid this tough." She stopped short of saying that sometimes she worried that Jennifer didn't feel pain or maybe that pain made her go, for fear of what Scotty might do with it in print.

"How do you mean?"

"Well, you saw her just now. She'll take a charge from *anyone*. Any size. I'll bet she draws more charging fouls than any two players in the league simply because she's willing to take a full shot," Kathy said, thinking how sometimes she worried that she couldn't coach Jennifer to protect herself better—put her hands up at least.

Out on the court the girls ran quarter-, half-, and full-court sprints alternately, and Jennifer Lawless led them all by a furlong, her face impassive, showing no sign of the burning pain in her legs and lungs.

"Word has it she's not bad on the academic front, too. Is that right?" Wakefield asked.

Boy, this guy is one incisive interrogater, Kathy thought. Saying Jen is "not bad" on the academic front is like saying Jerry Falwell trifles in fundamental Christianity. "Close to a four-point," Coach said patiently. "She's a National Merit Scholar finalist and probably the only athlete in school who's won a letter in every sport every year, two years at her old school in the Midwest and now two years here. I wish we'd had her all four years." At this point the coach's demeanor became exaggeratedly expansive as she stretched her arms out over the gymnasium floor, teasing Wakefield. "As far as her total high school record goes, Jennifer Lawless's sweat smells like a blend of the finest French perfumes." She dropped her hands and looked back at Wakefield. At the end of the bench Dillon Hemingway, applying reinforcing tape to a second stringer's ankle, raised his eyebrows in surprise and let out a loud guffaw.

"Can I quote that?" Wakefield asked.

"About her record," Coach Sherman said, "not about her sweat."

Wakefield smiled and shook his head, looking back to his notepad. "So, is she coachable?"

"Is a five-pound gerbil fat? The only problem I ever have is getting her to back off her intensity, and it's seldom you'll hear me complain about that."

Wakefield scribbled furiously for a few moments, then looked up to watch the action on the court. While fatigue, bordering on desperation, reigned prominently on the faces of the other players continuing the fierce conditioning drills, Jennifer clearly pulled away from them, seeming to gather energy rather than fade.

Visibly impressed, Wakefield turned back to the coach. "So, how do you plan to play Renee Halfmoon?"

"I don't plan to play Renee Halfmoon," Kathy answered patiently. "I plan to play Wênatchee."

"Coach, I realize you coach from a complete team concept and all that, but you must know this girl is almost impossible to stop."

"That may be so, but if we concentrate on one player, the rest of her team will kick our butts." Coach smiled and patted the reporter on the shoulder. "Listen, Scotty, write this down. We're a running team; they're a running team. They have one of the best athletes in the state, and we have one of the best athletes in the state, both at the same position. Either team would be in the top ten *without* Jen or Renee Halfmoon. If the teams are up and Renee and Jen are up, well, when Saturday night rolls around, you best wear your boots and bring your shootin' iron. Guaranteed."

Jennifer Lawless read her coach's comments in the *Free Press* and smiled. She read them again as she cut them out and placed them on her desk along with articles sent by relatives and friends from all over. It was as if every prep school sports reporter from either side of Washington State had discovered girls' basketball in the same week as Wakefield. This was only the halfway point in the season, but because of geography, it might be the only time all year that Chief Joseph and Wenatchee would play each other—her only shot at Renee Halfmoon. Jennifer looked forward to it like nothing so far in her life.

The knock on her bedroom door froze her insides, as always, and she hesitated before answering, in as near normal a voice as she could. "Who goes?"

"I goes," came the answer. Her sister, Dawn. "Can I come in?"

"Sure. Just a sec." Jennifer got up from the desk and moved to the latch on the door. "Give me the password," she teased.

"What password? There's no password."

"That's it," Jennifer said through the door and flipped the latch.

Dawn slipped in, saw the articles on the desk, and moved directly to them, touching them lightly, reverently. "It's like you're famous."

"A little," Jennifer replied. She watched Dawn's eyes, looked at the wonder, wishing there weren't quite so much worship, but embracing it at the same time.

"Think you guys can win this game?" Dawn asked.

"Um-hmm," Jen said, "I think us guys can win this game."

Dawn looked back at the articles a little longer, moving them around. She had none of Jen's physical toughness, as much lighter in build as she was darker in color. Dawn was the princess of the family, and Jen feared for her. "Is this Halfmoon chick as good as you?"

"She's better than me."

Dawn's head shot up. "Oh, no sir," she said. "She's not better. No one in the state's better. It says so right here in this story." She pointed to one of the clippings.

"Renee Halfmoon is," Jennifer said casually. "I've seen her play. There's nothing she can't do. She's as sweet as anyone I've seen, boys or girls."

"Yeah, but she's not better than you," Dawn insisted. "Look." She pointed again to the clippings.

"Dawn," Jennifer said impatiently, "most of the people who wrote those articles haven't seen both of us play, and none of them has seen us play each other. Wait till you see her. I mean, God, she's *liquid*."

"She's still not better than you." Dawn wouldn't give it up.

"Okay, little sis." Jennifer gave in. "She's not better

than me. Tell me about seventh grade. You knockin' 'em dead?"

"If she's better than you," Dawn said, unable to let this bad news pass, "how come there's all this newspaper and TV stuff? And how come you said you guys will win?"

"Because she's *better.* I'm *tougher.* Because the only people in the world who know she's better are you and me. And when it's all over, we'll still be the only ones. Now how are things in junior high? You knockin' 'em dead?"

Going into the fourth quarter of the Wenatchee game the score is dead even, and the Coliseum pulsates with intensity. Every word written by every would-be Ring Lardner from the weekly wheat town rags to the *Seattle Times* has come true. The two top triple A girls' teams in the state have just completed three quarters of the best run-and-gun basketball seen in Washington in a decade, with no hint of a letup.

Jennifer Lawless sits on the bench, a wet towel draped over her head, listening to Coach Sherman map out the last quarter.

"Okay, listen," she says with a smile. "This is what it's all about. From here on only one team in the state finishes on a win. They're good. They're in good shape. They ain't gonna fold, ladies. You're gonna have to go after this one."

The players sit forward. "Yeah! Come on! Let's get this! Let's put it away!"

"Okay," Kathy says. "That's what I wanna hear. Now you gotta pressure them. After every score, go to the full-court press. No score, go to the half-court. We're hanging with them fine, so we'll stay in a man-to-man. Don't get too eager and watch the fouls, but play *tight*. If you get tired, pat your head and we'll get someone in there for you. We can't stop Halfmoon's shot, so we're going to have to deny her the ball. Make 'em work for every pass. Nothing easy. Jen, you've got only one foul, so get on her like a bad smell."

Jennifer nods from beneath the towel. She's concentrating, thinking ahead to Renee's moves, seeing herself get in front to block her off, make her take the bad shot or trap her down low. So far it's been a standoff; Renee's hitting everything she throws up from outside, but Jennifer's stopping her underneath for the most part. Jennifer's outside shot is off; but she's had a spectacular inside game, and she's controlling the boards like she'd built them, so the superstars have represented an astonishing but equal trade-off. Jennifer pulls the towel down farther over her head and forces everything else out. That's what Jennifer Lawless is good at—forcing things out.

The fourth quarter continues at a killing pace, the momentum slipping back and forth like liquid mercury under a squeegee. Neither team can get up by more than four points, and with a minute and a half remaining, Coach Sherman calls for time, down by two. "Okay," she says, "slow it down just a little. We've got the ball, so work for a good shot. Go with number three on the inbound. Jen, you can get loose by the side of the key if you're quick. Take it underneath. Your outside shot has seen better days. . . ."

Jennifer nods without speaking, blocking out everything but the move, watching herself make it again and again between now and the time she'll actually execute it.

"Think we can win this one?" Coach asks.

"Yes!"

"Okay. Get in there and put it away. I'm tired and I want to go home."

The players join hands in the center of the huddle, jerk them up and down in unison, yelling, "Kick ass!" in a meter that sounds more like "Ki-kass" and can't be picked up by the fragile sensibilities of the crowd, and walk to their positions.

At the whistle Jennifer takes Renee down low, then cuts back to receive the pass, shaking her for the split second it takes to get free. She starts a move to the hoop but is blocked and passes back out quickly. Vickie Knight, Chief Joe's point guard, takes it back up top and sets up, calling a number and looking for an inside pass. She's trapped, and Jennifer comes up top to help, gets the pass, and instantly drives to the hoop, catching Renee Halfmoon off guard for a split second, driving behind her to the baseline for a short jumper that barely disturbs the net. Chief Joe goes immediately into a full-court press, and Wenatchee can't fast-break, instead bringing the ball up slowly amid the deafening roar from the crowd and tremendous court pressure. Renee Halfmoon works her side of the court, trying to shake Jennifer, but Jen fights her way through two poorly set screens, denying Renee any chance at the ball. Wenatchee's point guard drives toward the hoop and dishes off to the forward on the other side. Out of the corner of her eye Jen sees her own teammate beaten and slides over to help. Renee moves outside and is free to receive the pass and, in the same fluid movement, pops a jumper to put Wenatchee up again by two.

Jen takes a chance as the ball leaves Renee's hand and breaks for the opposite basket while Vickie snatches it out of the net, steps out, and fires a perfect strike to her on the fly. Wenatchee's point guard streaks after her but has no chance, and Jen goes up untouched for the easy two, tying the score with less than thirty seconds to play, and Chief Joe's players walk over to Coach Sherman for some of that late-game magic that got them here.

Only in concentration is there magic. "Just don't give them a good shot and don't foul. They have to be hitting at least seventy-five percent from the line. Let's don't lose this on a freebie. They'll go to Halfmoon. Jen, stay on her. If she gets the ball, whoever's close give Jen some help. No room for mistakes here, ladies. In thirty seconds either we'll have our excuses or we'll have this game."

The buzzer sounds, and the players take their spots. Wenatchee gets the ball in easily and brings it up slowly, once again under tremendous pressure, working down those last agonizing seconds. Each of Chief Joe's players is glued to her man, and Wenatchee works furiously to get someone open on picks but is shut off. With eight seconds remaining, Rence Halfmoon breaks for the hoop up high behind her high post's perfectly set screen on Jen, and Jen spins off to catch her. For a second it appears Renee has her beaten, but Jen miraculously slides to a spot between Renee and the hoop and plants herself. An astonished Renee desperately strains to switch direction at the same time that she pulls up short to avoid the charging foul; but it's too late, and she flips the ball underhanded toward the hoop. It bounces straight back at them off the front of the rim, striking the court at their feet, headed for out-of-bounds. Both girls dive, neither sure who touched it last, and Jen is able to get her fingertips on it a split second before Renee crashes off-balance into her legs, and the crowd rises in unison to the sound of Jen's head cracking against the hardwood like a cantaloupe dropped from the rafters. The ref's whistle calling a loose ball foul on Renee Halfmoon and the game-ending buzzer sound together, and with both teams in the penalty situation, Jen is about to get a chance few athletes ever get and, truth be told, few want. She struggles to her feet; but the court and the crowd and the players spin as if in a slow-motion food processor, and she sinks back to the floor. The players gather around her, followed closely by Dillon Hemingway, the trainer, pushing his way through, kneeling and sticking three fingers in front of her face. "How many?" he yells over the crowd.

Jennifer slaps his hand away. "I can see," she lies. "Just give me a sec."

Dillon looks back to Coach Sherman, who is still on her way, and waves her back to the bench.

There is no time on the clock as Jen stands at the top of the key alone. Players from both teams stand behind her, awaiting the outcome of their season, which rests unconditionally on Jen's ability to drop a freebie under pressure. There will be no rebound, no last-second desperation jumper, but none of that is clear to Jen, whose brain is swimming. She bounces the ball slowly, shaking her head, willing away the throbbing pain deep in the rear of her skull and forcing together as one the two hoops she sees floating before her. Jennifer Lawless has made a living out of free throws all season long, and she has yet to give in to pressure of any kind, and she won't now if she can just focus on the rim. She shakes her head again, bouncing the ball deliberately, buying precious seconds, and blocking out the screaming crowd. She holds the ball a second longer, then lets it go as darkness crowds in. She does not see it snap the bottom of the net, nor does she hear the Chief Joseph fans erupt.

CHAPTER 3

Jennifer tried to lift her head from the pillow, but the throbbing pain forced it back. Lights flashed across the ceiling and walls, and a vaguely familiar silhouette sat motionless against the window to her left. It took her a moment to realize the wail of the siren came from the vehicle in which they rode. Slowly the evening's events crept back into her head. She squinted again at the figure in the window and realized it was her sister, Dawn. Tears streamed down Dawn's face as she stared silently out the window. Jen felt a hand on her head, looked up and behind her to see Coach Sherman, sitting next to Dillon.

"Nasty spill," the coach said, and Dawn's head snapped around, relief pouring almost instantly over her face. She leaned over and hugged Jen, then buried her face in Jen's shoulder.

Jennifer looked back up at her coach. "Did it go in?"

"Yes indeedy, it did," Kathy said.

Jen pushed back into the pillow. "Thought so." She rubbed the back of Dawn's head as Dawn held tightly to her. "Hey, little sis, what's the matter with you? I got a bump on the head, is all."

Dillon reached over and put a hand in the middle of Dawn's back. "Yeah," he said. "A bump. About the size of an avocado."

"I thought you were dead," Dawn sputtered into Jen's shoulder. "I was yelling at you and you wouldn't answer. I thought you were dead."

Coach Sherman laughed. "She *was* yelling at you. Would've woke *me* up."

"Next time," Jennifer said to Dawn, "put a mirror under my nostrils."

"What?"

"If it fogs up, I'm still alive."

Dawn was feeling better, raised her head, and sat back on the ambulance seat. "Hey," she said, "it's not funny. I thought something was really wrong."

Jennifer flashed on what that could mean for Dawn if it were true. She was relatively certain Dawn didn't know all—knew the violence, but not the rest.

"Well, nothing's really wrong." She looked to her coach. "Hey, Coach, I'm okay, right? I mean, I won't have to stay at the hospital or anything, right?"

"Do you see my medical degree hanging anywhere on the wall?" Kathy asked. "I don't have any idea. But if the doctor says you stay, you stay. We couldn't get hold of your parents, so I have the say, understood?"

"I feel fine," Jennifer said. "Really. I don't want to stay overnight, okay?"

"It's okay that you don't want to," Kathy said. "But it doesn't mean you won't."

The ambulance pulled up to the emergency door at Sacred Heart Hospital, and in seconds the back doors swung open and medics swooped Jennifer out.

Following a relatively short wait, lying flat on an examination table, staring into a bright light, Jen heard the door open and the ER doctor step quietly into the room. He looked over the paperwork her coach had filled out with Jen's help upon entry, then walked over and stood above and behind her. Jen knew from reading his nametag upside down that his name was Christian.

"Hi," Jen said. "I can't stay."

"Is that right?" Dr. Christian answered flatly. "Guess we shouldn't have sent out for Chinese."

"Guess not. Really, I have to go home. There's no one to take care of my sister."

"How 'bout you let me examine your gourd before we waste time on an argument we may not need to have?" the doctor said.

"Okay, I'll shut up. But I can't stay."

Dr. Christian proceeded to shine his light into Jen's eyes, asking her sometimes to follow it and sometimes to look straight at a point in front of her. He mumbled a couple of medical *mmm-hmm*s before asking her to sit up. As she made the attempt, the room immediately spun, and nausea swelled in her stomach; but she held on. Dr. Christian watched her sway, a little annoyed she would not be straight with him, then asked her to stand. Jen tried to keep up the charade but, as she stood, felt an overwhelming urge to vomit. She choked it back, one hand grasping the examination table.

"Let your hand fall free, please," Dr. Christian said, and Jen complied. The doctor caught her under the arms as her knees buckled. "Can't see any problem here," he said sarcastically. "Why don't you just trot along home?"

"Funny man," Jen said as he laid her head back down on the examining table. "What's wrong?"

"Probably a moderate concussion," he said. "I'm

sorry, young lady, but I can't grant your request for a pass. We need to keep an eye on you until this dizziness goes away, and we'll need to keep you awake for a while. If no one's at your house, there's no way I can allow you to go there."

"My sister's there."

"How old's your sister?"

"Twelve."

"Sorry, Charlie," Dr. Christian said, "StarKist wants tunas that are thirteen—"

"You don't understand."

"Yes, I do," he said, looking again at the chart. "I understand you want to go home. It's you who doesn't understand. You're not going." He looked at his clipboard. "Who's Kathy Sherman?"

"My coach."

"She brought you in?"

"Yeah."

The doctor disappeared for a few seconds, returning with Kathy and Dawn, explaining the situation on the way. Dillon remained in the waiting room.

"You're here for at least twelve hours," Kathy said. "Don't worry. I'll let your parents know what happened when I take Dawn home. They'll probably want to come see you."

Jen's throat closed as her mind raced. She was caught. There was no way out of here tonight. She hated her body for betraying her but knew she couldn't make it to the door if her life depended on it. "Okay," she said. "But could I talk to you alone for a minute, Coach?"

"Sure," she said, glancing at the doctor and Dawn, motioning them with her eyes toward the door.

"We'll be right out here," Dr. Christian said. "I'll get someone going on your room."

When the door closed, Jen took a deep breath and closed her eyes. "Coach, could you do me a *big* favor?"

"If I can."

"Could you not call again? Take Dawn home with you, just for tonight?"

"Jennifer, I can't do that. What would your parents do if neither of you came home tonight and no one told them why? Besides sue my ass off, I mean."

"They won't sue," Jennifer said. "Just take her home with you, okay?"

"Jen, what's this all about?"

"I can just tell you it's really important," Jen said. "*Really* important. They're probably not home yet anyway. You could say you called and no one answered. You could say I gave you the wrong number."

"Jen, this is a little strange. . . ."

"I know it's strange, but could you? Just this once?"

Coach Sherman searched Jennifer's eyes for a clue to the sense of this but saw only the urgency. Truth was, this kid could get almost anything she wanted from Kathy. Jen was the most easily coached kid she'd had, and her intensity reminded her of a young Kathy Sherman. She was aware that alone bought Jen extra room with her. Not that she needed it. "Okay, I'll take her home. But I have to call in the morning. And if you're going to ask me to do things like this, I'm going to expect an explanation sometime in the near future."

"Thanks," Jen said, and closed her eyes.

Knowing Dawn was with Coach Sherman released Jennifer into a warm, half-conscious state as she lay back to await being transferred to a room. Vaguely aware of her damp, cold uniform covered only by her warm-up top, and her hair matted against her forehead with sweat, she drifted, floating weightlessly back to the last time in her life she really felt safe—felt as if she didn't have to be suspect of everything around her.

She's five. Her grandfather is there, sitting in his overstuffed chair with a storybook in his lap, a Dr. Seuss book. . . .

"C'm'ere, J. Maddy. Let Grampa read you some poetry," and Jen automatically glances up in delight. "This here's *real* poetry. None of them 'silver bells and cockled shells' an' the rest of that foolishness."

To Jennifer and Grampa, *real* poetry means Horton. Or the Long Legger Kwongs from *Scrambled Eggs Super*, or Bartholomew Cubbins' five hundred hats. Jennifer slides across the room and crawls up into her grandfather's lap, leaning in against his soft red plaid flannel shirt, which smells of cherry pipe tobacco and car engine grease, easily the best-combined olfactory experiences in existence to a five-year-old girl who worships the old man who always keeps her safe and always reads *real* poetry.

"Now, J. Maddy, you can read right along with me if you want," Grampa says. His voice is rich and deep, and he talks in a slow drawl, though there is nothing southern in his history. He's a big man, with a huge, round head full of silver hair and a handlebar mustache. His fingers are short and thick, with dirt under the nails, always dirt under the nails, which Gramma complains about night and day, but which Jennifer considers part of Grampa's fingers.

"You're gettin' right smart for your age," Grampa

says, then laughs. "And for your breeches, too. So if you wanna read along, you go right ahead." He calls her J. Maddy because her middle name is Madeline—his own sister's name—and he put up a pretty good fight for an old man in the hospital five years ago, when his son and daughter-in-law were filling out the birth certificate, to have Jen's first and middle names in the reverse order of what they wanted, but he lost in the end, as he always does in this family. He wanted her named after his sister because she had been the only human being on the face of the earth he really trusted. She was gone now, and he hoped he could re-create that trust with his granddaughter, the way he failed to do with his wife and family.

The trust is there, and to him Jennifer is J. Maddy.

"Sighed Mayzie, a lazy bird hatching an egg:
'I'm tired and I'm bored
And I've kinks in my leg
From sitting, just sitting here day after day.
It's work! How I hate it.
I'd *much* rather play. . . .'"

Jennifer reads right along with Grampa. She doesn't really recognize many of the words by sight, but she's heard Horton's saga of hatching Mayzie's egg so many times she can say it in her sleep.

«‹‹›››

"We're moving you now." A nurse, one Jennifer hadn't seen before, touched her gently on the forehead. "I want you to slide off the table and sit in this wheelchair, okay?"

Jennifer opened her eyes, unable to tell if she had been asleep or simply daydreaming. Seconds passed before she realized where she was. Grampa was *so* real. "Yeah, sure," she said after a moment, and sat up slowly, then eased herself down into the chair. The dizziness seemed to have passed, and the maneuver was not difficult.

She was being moved to a private room because it was the only one available, the nurse explained, and because they intended to wake her up periodically during the evening to check her responses.

The nurse was out of the room only seconds before . . .

«‹‹›››

Jennifer is back in her grandfather's lap, clapping with glee as the egg hatches and out flies a miniature elephant with wings, an exquisite replica of Horton himself, his reward for patience and tenacity through what could only be described as pachyderm hell.

Jennifer's dad, her *real* dad—who appears in her dreams and fantasies only as a shadow, with no real face or weight or size—lurks in the kitchen doorway and watches them read. A coldness washes over Jen, and she moves tighter into Grampa's flannel shirt, concentrates harder on Horton's delight and Mayzie's rage, as if to wipe out her father's presence. She does not know he will be out of her life very soon, only to be replaced by something worse. Only with Grampa is she safe.

"You're spoiling that girl rotten," says Jen's grandmother from the front porch. "You won't live forever, you know. What's she gonna do when you're gone? I can't be reading to her twenty-four hours a day, and neither can her mother. Who even knows if her father can read?" These last words—the words about her father—are spit out with such contempt they feel like arrows to Jennifer.

Grampa is always short with Gramma. It seems the only way to protect himself from her poisonous tongue. There is little warmth between them even in the best of times, little warmth anywhere in the family, really. "Can't be done," Grampa says. "Can't spoil a five-year-old. Not with time. Not with love." He shakes his head.

"Can't be done." He runs his thick fingers through Jennifer's hair, smiles his tired smile, and whispers, "Don't ever believe that. Anytime anyone tries to spoil you, just soak it up. You hear?"

Jennifer smiles secretly at him and nods. Though she can't put words to the feelings, she senses that her days of being "spoiled rotten" by Grampa are numbered. She has seen him do strange things lately, things that cause the rest of the family to look at each other and shake their heads behind his back. Yesterday at lunch Grampa put chicken gravy on his ice cream. Jen started to laugh—she thought Grampa was making a joke—but he looked so confused it scared her and she didn't tell him. *He thinks it's potatoes,* Jen thought when she saw him pour the full ladle of gravy over his dessert; *he just forgot.* But then he ate it. *He must think those are awful cold potatoes,* she thought, but she couldn't shake the idea that something was going wrong with Grampa. Not long ago he got lost coming home from the store, and the police brought him back. Jen watched him get out of the police car and stand at the end of the walk, looking confused, and she ran out to him, yelling and squealing, and that brought him right back. She does that sometimes, and sometimes it works. She makes loud noises when he seems confused.

But he's okay way more than he's not okay, and Jen sees it as her job to help him when she can.

Now Grampa stands in the middle of a field. They live in Lawrence, Kansas, and springtime has created a rich greenness that stretches forever. Towering, white billowy clouds fill the deep blue sky, and the sun shines brightly on his silver hair. Jennifer stands watching him, edging closer as she glimpses the shadow that is her father on the horizon. It is a pathetic shadow, but also giant somehow, one that fills her from inside, chokes her. Grampa stands tall in the field with a beveled wooden object hanging from his hand. Jennifer recognizes from Grampa's exaggerated pomp that this is yet another of the toys that will be named after her, like J. Maddy Yo-Yo and J. Maddy Hula-Hoop (which Grampa can skid almost halfway across the lawn and make return on its own English). These are all toys that go away and come back.

"This is J. Maddy Boomerang," Grampa says. "J. Maddy Boomerang, I want you to meet J. Maddy Lawless."

J. Maddy Lawless says hi.

J. Maddy Boomerang hangs from Grampa's hand.

"J. Maddy Boomerang," Grampa continues, "flies far and free. She flies up to the clouds, *past* the clouds to the other side of the moon, where princesses are monsters and monsters are friends. They tease her and terrify her and tickle her silly."

Jennifer is mesmerized by Grampa's nonsensical tale, as she always is, staring at J. Maddy Boomerang hanging innocently at his side.

"And then she flies home, where it's safe and warm and there's plenty of Ho-Hos and Ding-Dongs and chocolate-covered grasshoppers."

"Oooooh." Jen wrinkles her nose. "Chocolate *grasshoppers*? She eats grasshoppers?"

"She surely do," Grampa says, and with a flip of his elbow and wrist he sends the boomerang spinning forward, climbing, climbing toward the majestic clouds. Jennifer watches in amazement as it starts back toward them in a wide arc. Grampa moves close to protect her, and together they watch it dig into the dirt less than ten yards from where they stand. Jennifer cheers and runs to retrieve it. They repeat the story and the act, and Jennifer helps Grampa make up new creatures for the kingdom on the other side of the moon. She tries throwing the boomerang herself a few times but is quickly stymied.

The ghostly presence of her father sits on the horizon like a dull ache on the edges of her consciousness.

It's night—very late at night—when Jennifer's father creeps into her room. She can't remember when it started—can't remember the first time. Maybe he has always come, though now he stays longer. She lies awake, dreading the faint creak of the door, followed by the soundless sensation that someone is very near. She feels his pressure on the end of the bed and waits through the silence until he chooses to talk. This is why she tries to stay with Grampa most of the time. But there are always times when she can't work it out, can't get Gramma to let her stay there, or can't get Grampa to stay at her house. When she can, she keeps him up very late—until after her folks go to bed—playing and reading stories. Often then he falls asleep on her bed and she sleeps easy, sheltered. But Grampa isn't here tonight. Daddy is. And Daddy starts to talk. Jennifer doesn't really understand all his words, but he talks about her body, and he tells her he loves her a lot, but it doesn't feel like it does when Grampa says it. It feels good—kind of—in a strange sort of way, but it also feels icky. Daddy seems like a little boy now, really, and he puts his hands up inside Jennifer's nightgown and touches her in places that her mother calls "privates" when she washes them in the bathtub. It feels awful to be touched there, but it feels good to make Daddy feel good; any other time he almost never does. And it's a secret. Jennifer is very good at keeping secrets. It's her very best thing, Daddy says. It's something we can never tell or Mommy will get very sick and people will come and take Jennifer away. She wants to tell. If she told someone, it would be Grampa, but this is really the only warm feeling she has with anyone in her family except him. It's the only time Daddy seems to love her.

«‹‹»›»

"Jennifer. Jennifer." The voice came from far away, and Jennifer struggled to bring it into focus. "I need to look in your eyes again, all right, Jennifer?" A dim light—probably a night-light—illuminated the room, and a woman in white stood over her with a small penlight. Jennifer remembered where she was and rested back against the pillow. She told the nurse to go ahead, following the instructions to the letter.

"Your eyes are dilating about the way they should be now," the nurse said. "I probably won't be waking you again."

Jennifer nodded and said that would be a relief. "If

they stay that way, can I get out of here tomorrow?" she asked.

"I'm sure you can," the nurse answered. "We just wanted to be sure you weren't going to have any difficulty. You took a pretty hard hit, they tell me."

«‹›»

Sitting beside Grampa on the big couch at his house, Jennifer attempts to put together a Dumbo the Elephant puzzle. The puzzle has more than fifty pieces and is, in fact, too complex for her, but the pieces seem to materialize very close to where they belong whenever she gets stuck. Grampa tells her she must be a born puzzle fixer. "We're here at ABC's Wide World of Puzzles," he says in his best Howard Cosell voice, "and young J. Maddy Lawless is attempting to put together the never-before-assembled Dumbo Circles High Above the Big Top, a six-*quadrillion*-piece monster of a puzzle that has baffled experts in seven countries and fourteen tropical islands."

"Grampa, you talk funny," Jennifer says as an all-gray piece of Dumbo's ear appears magically by her finger, less than an inch from where it belongs. "You sound like that guy that talks on TV. The one at Monday football."

"Yes, I do," Grampa says, slipping into his W. C.

Fields, but then he stops, a little dazed, and looks at Jennifer, reaching across his body with his right hand to his left, massaging a bit, looking puzzled.

"Say some more, Grampa," Jennifer says. "Say some more about what a great puzzle lady I am. Put me on television some more."

Grampa looks bewildered now, feels his arm again, and shakes his head. He moves his hand tentatively back to the puzzle pieces but only fingers them absently. He hears a buzzing sound, then is smashed with a hammer to the chest. "J. Maddy . . ." he starts again in Cosellese, but it trails off. Then: "J. Maddy, you go get your mother, okay? Go get her and tell her Grampa needs to see her right away."

"I think she went to the store. She said she'd be back in—"

"J. Maddy, you go get your momma now, you hear? You go get your momma and tell her to come right in here, okay, J. Maddy?"

Jennifer looks into Grampa's eyes, but he's not in there. He's not looking very far past his face, and he's rubbing one arm with the other hand, then clutching at his chest. He blinks twice, but Jennifer doesn't think he sees anything.

"She's at the store, Grampa," Jennifer says, and

now she's getting scared. "Grampa, are you all right? Are you all right, Grampa?"

"J. Maddy," he says; but Jennifer can see he's not really talking to her, and he grabs his chest and slumps to the side. She crawls quickly across the coffee table, knowing something is terribly wrong, and she'll never get this puzzle together without him, that she won't be safe. . . .

Jennifer stands on the couch and braces herself under Grampa's shoulder, trying to push him back up. She knows if she can sit him upright, like he was a minute ago, he'll be okay. But the weight . . .

He seems to fold over her when she pushes, engulfs her, so she crawls across his lap to the other side and tries to pull him up by his left shoulder. It doesn't work, but she's *sure* if she can just get him upright, get him sitting. Like he was . . .

It's fifteen or twenty minutes before Jennifer is able to get Grampa sitting up. Her tiny body is soaked with sweat from trying to perform this impossible task, but never once does she think to go for help. It doesn't occur to her that anyone in the family would want to help. Grampa has always been hers, like she is his. They are two people at far ends of the spectrum, and they don't matter in this house, unless, of course, you count when

Mommy wants her to show off how smart she is or that late-night time when her daddy sneaks into her room. That matters. . . .

For more than a half hour Jennifer remains wedged against Grampa's ribs, propping him up in his sitting position. She continues with the puzzle, at least the parts she can reach, and Grampa is long gone. Jennifer talks to him as if he were still there, magically guiding her hands to the right places with the right pieces; but the going is slower, and several pieces have been forced into the wrong spots. "Does this one go here?" she asks patiently, waiting about the right amount of time for an answer, then: "Guess not, maybe here." Tears stream down her face, but she refuses to let what is real be real. When Grampa's gone, well, who knows what when Grampa's gone?

It all falls apart when Jennifer's mother walks into the room from the kitchen, where she has just set down two sacks of groceries on the counter. She is talking as she walks through the door, though Jen has no idea what she's saying. There is dead silence, then a muffled shriek as her mother sees Grampa's dead eyes staring somewhere off the arm of the couch, his face ashen.

"Jennifer! Jennifer!" her mother yells at her, but Jennifer stares valiantly at the puzzle, trying to figure how the feather goes into Dumbo's trunk. "Jennifer, your granddad . . ."

Jen stares harder at the puzzle.

Her mother takes Jen by the waist and pulls her away from the couch, and Grampa slumps over. Jen automatically moves back to try to prop him up, but her mother snatches her again by the waist and points her toward the door. "You go outside, dear," she says desperately. "I'll see to Grampa."

Jen turns on her mother then, eyes blazing, defiant. "You won't see to Grampa," she says between gritted teeth, her hands locked onto her hips, upper body protruding over her legs so far as to defy gravity. "You won't see to Grampa. Grampa's dead. He's dead. Nobody ever sees to Grampa." Her mother's hand flashes out and slaps her hard across the face. The tears and the snot begin to run then, but Jen holds her ground. "And nobody ever sees to me!" she yells, and runs out of the room.

Her mother stands stunned, as usual, totally ineffectual at dealing with either crisis. She turns to her father's corpse. . . .

Jennifer feels the steel casing start to form around her heart from her perch in the tree just outside the back porch. First her father comes home, sees her there but makes no acknowledgment and disappears into the house. After her father come the fire department and a policeman. Grampa is taken away on a long bed with wheels, and his whole body is covered with a blanket. Jennifer can't see him, but she knows it's him. Then other people start to arrive; some she knows are aunts and uncles and cousins and some are just neighbors. Some she doesn't know at all. Several folks look at her up in the tree, and a few make feeble attempts at coaxing her down; but Jennifer will not budge. She will sit there well into the night.

If I could have sat him all the way up . . . she thinks. *If I could have sat him all the way up, I could have saved him.* She hates her mother for making her leave the room before they got the puzzle fixed. She was the only one in the world who really cared about Grampa. And the people who care about you are the only ones who can save you.

CHAPTER 4

Dear Preston,

Been thinking a *lot* since I wrote last. Funny, most of it's been about Stacy. My thoughts about her keep me in a constant state of confusion. I said before I hated that she loved you and not me, and that's not exactly true. I didn't hate that she loved you. I just hated that she didn't love me. I fell into the trap of believing that strong feelings about a person are exclusive of feelings about any others. That's what *they* tell us, but it's a lie. The part of Stacy that liked me and talked with me and was intimate in all those ways that aren't *man-woman* ways didn't have anything to do with you. And her love for you, her attraction and her sexual draw toward you, didn't have anything to do with me. I got them confused, I think; thought I couldn't have my part without your part. I'm sorry I was such a smartass all those times I said things like

"Why go for the Plymouth Duster when you can have the 'Vette?" I think that probably hurt you a lot because you believed the analogy. And truth be known, I probably did, too. I have some things to learn about unwarranted arrogance. I keep going back to this time I ran into her at the carnival. You might remember, it was the time I lost Christy and ended up spending three life sentences grounded to my room. I play it over like it happened yesterday—don't have a clue why it's important except that it tells me something about my roots with her and why she seems so important in my life.

She hollers, "Wait up!" from around the corner, just back from the bottle throw. I hear her, recognize her voice, but I can't see her through the crowd. "Wait!" she yells again, so I stand fast, holding Christy by the back of her coat collar, letting Stacy find me.

"Look!" she yells, and finally I see her, sidestepping all the folks pressed up to the dart throw, dancing through the steady stream of people moving toward the big green canvas tent for the next performance of EPHRAIM, THE ASTOUNDING DOG BOY, THE ONE AND ONLY OF HIS KIND IN THE WESTERN HEMISPHERE.

I wonder if they have an abundance of astounding dog boys in the *Eastern* Hemisphere.

"Dillon," she hollers again, waving with one hand,

pointing at me with the other, this funny-looking, colored straw extension protruding from her index finger, aimed directly at my heart.

I say, "Hi," as Christy reaches for the sky like a saloon bartender robbed by the Daltons, and drops to her knees, sliding out of her coat and my grasp. I dive and catch her belt loop an instant before she could have scrambled into the crowd, only to surface at Lost and Found a half hour later stuffed with ice cream and cotton candy to silence her wailing until Mom or I got there. Part of me wants to let her go because though I'm only nine years old, I'm totally, hopelessly, irrevocably in love with Stacy Ryder and I know I could negotiate those mysterious waters better without my pain-in-the-butt sister in the boat. But I am what Mom calls a "trustworthy caretaker," and besides, Stacy likes *you*, so I don't let Christy go. "Nice try, peckerbrains," I say, lifting her to her feet by the belt and handing her jacket back. "Put this back on. Don't make me use the leash."

Christy's eyes narrow defiantly, and that impish smile crosses her lips, letting me know that wasn't her last, or even her best, escape attempt. I don't know how we were able to keep her in the family, Pres. Seems like she spent her first ten years trying to get away. Maybe she knew something we didn't.

"Stick your finger in here," Stacy says, and I stare at the long orange-and-brown woven straw barrel extending from the end of her finger like a silencer on a handgun.

"What is it?"

"Just stick your finger in."

I hesitate, squinting. "Is this a trick?"

She raises her eyebrows, a move I have long been convinced was designed solely to bring me to my knees. "Of course, it's a trick," she says. "This is a carnival."

I stick my finger in. "Gotcha," she says. "You can't get away."

This is Stacy Ryder. I don't *want* away, but I pull my hand back anyway. The straw tightens around my knuckle. I pull harder.

"Pull as hard as you want," she says. "It won't come off."

I do pull harder, yank it, but my finger is caught fast. "What is this thing?" I ask, bringing it, along with Stacy's hand, closer to my face.

She says, "Chinese handcuffs. Neat, huh?"

"Yeah, neat. Do the Chinese use these?"

"I guess. They're Chinese handcuffs."

"How do I get them off?"

She shrugs. "You don't. Once you're in 'em, you're in 'em for good. Unless you know the secret."

"So what's the secret?" I ask, at the same moment Christy drops out of the bottom of her jacket again. I reach; but Stacy and the Chinese handcuffs hold me back, and Christy stands just out of reach, hands on her buttocks, eyes squinted, chin stuck out a mile, a pose I'm sure you were as familiar with as I.

"You're in trouble now," she says, and vanishes in a forest of legs.

I say, "Shit. Lemme out of this, Stace. I gotta get her. God, my mom will kill me if she hears her name over the loudspeaker."

Stacy raises her eyebrows again and shrugs. "Sorry. You have to know the secret. The gypsy lady over by the Ferris wheel said it's a secret of life."

"My sister pay you?" I ask. Stacy does know the secret, and I know she knows the secret; but I'm aware there are worse things in life than being connected to Stacy Ryder for the rest of it, and *you're* not around to turn her head. And what the hell, Christy is long gone now anyway.

We wander around together for more than a half hour before Stacy finally shows me the secret, gently holding my hand in place at the wrist while she releases the pressure and slides her finger out; you've seen those things, right? Then she just looks at me innocently and shrugs, and I want instantly to lay down my life for her in some heroic and totally selfless way. But Christy has already been bailed out of Lost and Found by Mom, and *my* name is the one blaring over the loudspeaker every five minutes. Mom is searching furiously for me, intent on grounding me until my thirty-seventh birthday for turning a helpless five-year-old loose in such a dangerous place as the traveling carnival. I paid a lot of dues in my time for that little shit. I'm sure you did, too.

Anyway, to celebrate my liberation from the ridiculous handcuffs, which can't have cost more than three cents to make and whose secret of life is lost on me at the time, and to get in as much pleasure as I can before my impending incarceration, I take Stacy for two rides on the octopus and one on the hammer, leaving us nearly too sick to blow the rest of my money on hot dogs and cotton candy. No sense having cash during lifelong confinement. They have to feed you anyway.

I'm sure I have earlier memories of Stacy, Pres, but that's the one that always comes first. Being hooked to her and getting free of the handcuffs by releasing, instead of pulling hard. God, if I ever get *her* straight in my head, well, let's just say my life could take a turn for the simple. It was easier when you were still here because there was never any doubt who she was with. I grew up. I got bigger, I got stronger,

I may have even gotten smarter, but not smart enough to understand the effect she's always had on me. She may very well have been put on this planet by a sadistic, malevolent God to run my hormones wild and right into a brick wall and to make me feel truckloads of guilt for coveting the one thing my brother had that I wanted.

Boy, she was in love with you, Pres. She may have liked me better, but she loved you. I hated it. *I* saw her first. She was in *my* class at school. She copied off *my* homework. But she loved you. I tried to reason with her. By the time I was a sophomore and you were a senior, I had about an inch and fifteen pounds on you. That's when I started giving her the line about the Duster and the Corvette. That was cheap, Pres. I know it was.

She teased me back by asking why she should buy more car than she could use, but more or less wasn't really what it was all about. I don't want to be unfair or devalue what you guys had, but I think Stacy thought she could save you. I think that was a big part of her love. And I hate to say it, but I'm beginning to see that's a trick; it happens a lot, I think. Things get misnamed. Look what Mom and Dad called love.

It's hard for me to say these things, Preston, with you dead and all because it seems inequitable to pass judgment on your relationship with Stacy when you're not here to tell me I'm full of shit. But you left, and I'm stuck here to make sense of it, so I'm giving myself some leeway.

And speaking of your suicide, I haven't come completely clean to the rest of the world about it. And I don't know if I will. I even feel strange about writing it down. I've read too many stories about little sisters or moms, or whoever, finding diaries hidden in the dresser drawers underneath the underwear or back in the closet behind the shoes, but since there's no one alive to tell about it, I have to tell it to you just so I can look at it myself. Besides, when Mom hit the road, Christy went with her, and Dad wouldn't be caught dead in my room.

See, I might have known. I mean, when we got the guns and headed for the old cemetery, maybe I really knew you were going to do it. And if I *did* know, well, if I did know, then I'm the one who put the gun in your hands. Literally. Even as messed up as I'd seen you in your life, as broken down and scared and depressed and confused as you were when you first tried to kick the drugs, I'd *never* seen you like you were the day you shot yourself in the head. If a part of me knew, then another part wanted to let you go ahead. I mean, *I* wouldn't have wanted to live your life. The one crazy thing about being your brother and having you look so much like me—or vice versa, I guess you looked this way first—was that sometimes it was like seeing myself with everything off. You may well have been what I'd be were I stripped bare of my sense of humor and my willingness to fight; of my tenacity; even of my legs.

If my memory's right, it was the end of your junior year when you bought the Harley. God, I think you still had the first dollar you ever earned hauling groceries for that old woman down the block from us when you were seven. You could have had any bike you wanted with the bundle you had put away. I remember Mom and Dad almost crapped their drawers in parental crisis when you said you were going to get it, but you stood on the family rule that whatever money we kids earned was ours to do with as we pleased. I'll bet they'd change *that* one if they had it to do over again. I think it was meant for allowances, not ten-thousand-dollar savings accounts. I remember once he was resigned to the fact that his firstborn son and odds-on favorite to provide him grandchildren before fifty was going to be a biker, Dad tried to talk you into a Honda or Suzuki, because he saw the glaze in your eye every time you said the words *Harley-Davidson*, but you were dead set on that Sportster. God, and what a monster it was. I never did know much about motorcycles, as hard as you tried to educate me, but I didn't have to know much to know you were in front of me one second and a *long* ways down the road the next. And it sounded like you were strafing an airfield when you went by. This was one big, loud bike, my man.

I think Mom and Dad's anxiety went down a little after you'd been driving six months or so and your skin was still there to hold your body parts in, instead of laid out like a hairless bear rug on the freeway, but what they didn't know was you were busy connecting with the Warlocks. And as you well know now, no matter how sharp a bike you've got, there's only one way to hook up with the Warlocks if you're eighteen years old and 135 pounds, and that is to sell their wares.

At least they drummed out the jerk who steered you between those two semis. Your "initiation" move, right? God, Pres, you were smarter than that. You were. How bad did you want in with those creeps? You get to be a full member if you pulled off that move? Man, you must have been sky-high. Wolf himself told me you were crazy out of your gourd to follow Indian Red. Bikers may be a few bricks shy of a load sometimes, but they have more respect than that for hard pavement and fast trucks.

I've been thinking about the day you did it, Preston, and I gotta tell you, it rips up my insides, even now, but it also pisses me off so bad that if you hadn't succeeded, I'd probably have killed you. At least the way I feel today. I remember it like it was yesterday.

It was a day like few seen in Three Forks in February. At six-thirty in the morning the sky was clear as a bell with the temperature standing at forty degrees Fahrenheit. It would rise to sixty-one, a near record, before the afternoon sun slipped behind Boulder Peak. Winter had been mild, and there was little, if any, snow remaining on the ground. Outside, the light of dawn splashed a single streak of red in the eastern sky, the final evidence of the cloud cover passing over through the night, insulating the earth from the normal late-winter cold.

Dillon didn't normally get out of bed at six-thirty on a Saturday morning—in fact, he usually claimed ignorance of the fact that there *was* a six-thirty on Saturday morning—but on this day his eyes popped open as if by a secret alarm inside his head. He padded over to his bedroom window, pulling on his pajama bottoms, peering at the vague silhouette of Preston's van parked next to the garage, blocked by the shadow of the house from the early dawnlight. Initially Dillon thought Preston was leaving; but he heard the familiar sound of his wheelchair hitting the concrete, followed by the slam of the van door, and he knew Preston was just coming home. That could only mean trouble. He watched in silence as Preston wheeled himself slowly around the van, touching the hood ornament lightly, running his hand along the pinstriping and the dragon airbrushed onto the side door. Preston performed a couple of figure eights on the concrete driveway, shooting an imaginary ball at the hoop mounted on the backboard above the garage door, then wheeled over to the side of the house, just out of Dillon's sight. Dillon didn't know whether to leave him alone or go down and talk—Preston looked really peaceful from that distance—but he opted for the latter, because it all seemed so unusual, and because Preston's being out that late made him wonder if he'd been somewhere using again.

"Nice day," Dillon said from behind him, and Preston started slightly in the chair, not so much from being surprised as being brought back.

"Yeah."

"You just getting in?" Dillon asked.

"You my mother?"

No, you asshole, Dillon thought, *I'm not your mother. Your mother got sick of this crap and left, remember?,* but what he said was "Not the last time I looked."

"Then you don't need to know when I'm getting in."

Dillon backed way off. "I didn't mean to get nosy," he said. "I was just worried about you, that's all," and he turned to walk back into the house. "I just thought . . . Never mind."

Preston didn't respond.

Dillon knew there were going to be times when Preston was moody. He had refused to enter into any kind of drug treatment program, wanted to see if he could do it on his own first. "Sometimes when I'm hurtin'," he'd said at the outset, "I feel mean enough to kill, so those are probably good times to let me be." Dillon and his dad had agreed they would, but Dillon hadn't realized it would be so difficult. He had a temper, too, and his first reaction to being jumped on was to jump back, hard.

But on this day he walked back into the house.

Dillon's door cracked open like a gunshot two hours later, bringing him out of his bed like a sailor in a fire drill on a nuclear submarine. When his mind caught up, he saw Preston balanced on his back wheels in the bedroom doorway, a big smile plastered across his face. Seeing him like that, Dillon couldn't recall for certain whether their earlier encounter was real or a dream.

"Let's go shoot us some tin cans," Preston said.

"Some of my best friends are tin cans."

"All of your friends are tin cans. Let's go shoot some."

Dillon was aware this was the first time the two had joked around in a long time, maybe years, and he wasn't about to let it get away. He swung his legs over the edge of the bed as Preston dropped his front wheels back to the floor. "Meet me at the van in five," Preston said. "I got the shootin' irons."

Dillon was never much with a gun. That was his father's and Preston's territory. They were the hunters; he was the gatherer. He knew he'd probably drop a couple of Abe Lincolns or maybe even an Andrew Jackson on bets, as Preston fanned down a row of cans and bottles while *his* bullets strayed harmlessly into tree trunks and Mother Earth, but any connection was worth it. This was the first hint of anything that felt like *family* to him for a long, long time. It was only a crumb, but he'd had no idea how much he'd missed it.

Preston guided the van slowly up Cedar Street as Three Forks began to come alive. They stopped at Jackie's Home Cookin' for some pancakes and eggs, and Preston talked about old times—back *before* times—as he watched people passing by on the sidewalk from his window seat. "Remember when we were little and Dad used to take us on the mail run?" he asked, without waiting for an answer. "We'd come down here for breakfast really early in the morning and listen to the old neighborhood guys talk about shit they didn't know anything about, only we didn't know it.

God, I think the smell of this place is the best memory I have in the world." He was quiet a second, and Dillon started to answer, but Preston went on. "Sometimes we'd ask Stacy along and then fight about who she was with, remember?"

"She was with you," Dillon said.

Preston shook his head. "Man, I really messed that up."

Dillon wanted to say something about finally learning that Stacy would always be Preston's, no matter how much he wanted her to be his, and that he thought he'd finally let go of all that in the last year, but Preston started talking to the window again about buying the motorcycle to try to be a big shot and about losing his legs in the accident. He seemed so *empty*.

"Things would have been real different," Dillon said. "Some bad things happened that no one would have predicted."

"What are you talking about?" Preston said, and Dillon realized Preston wasn't aware he'd been talking aloud.

"You okay?" Dillon asked.

Preston came back. "Yeah, I'm okay. Tired, is all."

"Wanna go back home and catch some shut-eye? Gun down some tin cans later?"

Preston shook his head. "No. I'm not that tired. This is the day for it."

Dillon thought he meant shooting cans.

Preston pulled the van up next to the high old wooden fence surrounding the Crown Point Cemetery, about four miles outside the city limits. Crown Point had been the main graveyard in the 1800s, when Three Forks was a spot in the road rather than a budding city of two hundred thousand. Dillon reached into the back and hauled out Preston's chair, custom made of light alloy with special athletic wheels, carried it around the van, and opened it next to the driver's door. His dad and he had pooled their money and got it for Preston when he came home from the hospital in hopes that he'd get interested in wheelchair athletics. It didn't work. Preston played on a wheelchair basketball team for a little while, and he wasn't bad; but in a short period of time he secretly named it the Miami Express and started running drugs out of the Dragon tavern for the Warlocks. He had told Dillon at one point that the bartender in the Dragon checked a person's ID about once every third year, so he had no trouble coming and going from his new home base.

Preston extracted their grandfather's old German Luger out of the glove compartment and tucked it in his belt. For as long as Dillon could remember, Preston had kept that gun oiled and polished as if it were brand-new. Dillon collected both twenty-two rifles from the back and leaned them against the van before scouting the area for unsuspecting bottles and cans. Crown Point was a well-known make-out spot for Three Forks teenagers and offered up an abundance of beer and pop containers, and Dillon filled two empty cases with them while Preston wheeled the weaponry to a good flat spot from which to shoot.

While Dillon placed the targets carefully on tree stumps and fence posts and in the crooks of the branches of trees, Preston loaded the Luger's clip and filled the chamber of each of the rifles. Their game was simple: Choose a target; miss it and the points double for the other guy. No target was placed closer than thirty yards, and at least four of eleven were more than forty-five. Preston didn't miss one in the first round and finished it with a count of seven to Dillon's four. When Preston shattered a Bud bottle Dillon could barely see in the crotch of two large tree branches for his seventh to end the first round, Dillon hustled out to set up another eleven, thinking all the while how strange Preston was acting, how he kept shifting from loud and engaging to distant and silent. Preston had been silent throughout the last four shots.

"You feeling okay?" Dillon asked, walking back toward him from the tree where Preston had shattered the final Bud.

Preston had wheeled his chair nearly twenty feet from the spot they'd been shooting from, leaving the rifles back on the ground. The Luger was in his lap.

"Not tough enough, huh?" Dillon said. "Need a little bigger challenge?"

Preston picked up the pistol and fingered it slowly, looking down at it momentarily, then back at Dillon. Dillon thought for a split second Preston was going to shoot him. "Hey, Pres," he said, stopping at the rifles, "what's the matter?"

"A lot," Preston said. "A lot's the matter."

"What."

"Well, to start with," he said, picking up the gun in both hands and leveling it at one of the closer bottles, "you. You're the matter." He pulled the trigger, and the Luger jumped in his hands. The bottle nearly vaporized.

Dillon watched carefully, confused as to how he should feel, whether to be scared or not, as Preston leveled the gun again, this time kicking a can on the cemetery fence post ten feet into the âir. "What're you talking about?" Dillon said. "What do you mean *I'm* the matter?"

"I got to go out honest," Preston said. "If nothing else, I got to go out honest. Do you know what it's like watching what I could have been if I were big and strong and so goddamn *cool* all the time? So frigging *funny*?"

Dillon took a breath. "No, I guess I don't."

Preston nodded. "Nope. I guess you don't." He nailed a bottle at the edge of a ground squirrel hole. "Well," he said, "it ain't a lot of fun."

Dillon started toward him, but in that instant the barrel of the Luger was tight against Preston's temple. He said, "Stand fast, soldier."

Dillon stood fast. "Hey, Pres, you on something?"

Preston reached into his coat pocket and turned it inside out, dumping a mid-size street pharmacy onto the ground. "Yeah," he said, smiling, "I'm on a little something."

Dillon's throat knotted. He knew he might not have a chance to slow this down with Preston on drugs. He couldn't for the life of him predict Preston when he was high. For one thing he never knew what drugs Preston had taken, and even if he did, he'd never known all that much about the effects of drugs anyway.

"We can talk about this," he said.

"Oh, yeah, we can. We can talk about it." Preston lowered the Luger to his lap. "Go ahead, little bro. Go ahead and talk about it."

Dillon stood dumb, his heart pounding in his ears.

"At a loss for words?" Preston mocked. "You?"

Dillon said, "Yeah, I guess I am. I mean, I don't really know what's wrong, Pres. I didn't even know you were pissed at me."

Preston smiled and relaxed a trifle, and Dillon believed there *might* be a chance. "Ah, it's not just you. You're only a *little* of what's the matter, really. Got time for a story?"

"Yeah," Dillon said, moving a little closer, "I've got all the time you need."

In a flash the gun was back to Preston's temple. "Just sit tight," he said. "I can tell it from a distance."

Dillon stopped, and Preston lowered the gun again. "When I left last night, I was hating you bad. Both of you."

"Me and Dad?"

"You and Dad. I was sick of all the patronizing bullshit. All the goddamn *support*. All the time telling me I'm not the reason Mom and Christy left. Where'd you guys learn that stuff? You been talking to a shrink?"

Dillon said, "Dad talked to a drug counselor, I think. Hey, man, we didn't know what to do. You wouldn't go get any help or anything."

"Yeah, well, I was full up to about here of you guys," Preston said, measuring off a spot just under his chin to show exactly how full of them he was, "and thinking I'd been straight just about long enough. So I went over to the Dragon to look up a few of my old buddies. By the way, Dad'll be a little pissed when you get back. He's missing about three hundred bucks. Square it up for me, will you? Like, tell him I'm sorry."

"I'm not going back alone, Pres," Dillon said.

Preston smiled. "Oh, you're going back alone, all right. Unless you pick somebody up on the way."

Change swept over Preston before Dillon's eyes. The meanness drained out of him like dirty bathwater. "It's not you, Dillon. That was a bad rap. If it were, I'd shoot *you*. All you ever did was show me what I'm not." He was quiet for a long minute; Dillon stood frozen, realizing for the first time that Preston *really* meant to kill himself and that he had no chance of doing anything about it unless he could keep him talking until Preston came down from the drugs.

"There was a woman in the Dragon," Preston said,

and he was glazed over now. "A girl, really. I'd be surprised if she was seventeen. Nobody checks ID. She was crazy to be there. Everyone else was bikers and biker's mommas and dopers. The place was thick with meanness, and this girl was pushing it all the way, waving her boobs around like they were water balloons at a summer picnic, grinding her butt in the air over by the pool table. Picked herself up a following." Preston put the gun up to his temple and made a firing sound with his throat, as if in dress rehearsal, then rested it back in his lap.

"I had about a half dozen cross tops in me and a nose full of coke, washed down with a pitcher of Bud, and I was making a deal for a little crack—four months of clean living wiped out in fifteen minutes. And I tell you, little bro, being on shit is the only way I ever felt big. And I was feeling *big*.

"So somebody—hell, it might have even been me—said we oughta give this honey some of what she was asking for. It went up for a quick vote and came back by God unanimous. Wolf goes over and picks her up—she's squealing and pawing at him—and throws her on her back on the pool table; you heard her head hit. All of a sudden she's scared, real scared, starts to fight him, but hell, one of Wolf's *tattoos* weighs more than her whole self. He just pins her down by the throat with one hand and tears off her skirt and goes to town. And then they line up."

Preston stopped a second and lowered his head. Dillon quickly considered charging him to try to get the gun, but too much distance stood between them. And he knew he wouldn't get a second chance. Preston was serious.

"I watched it all," Preston said. "I cheered them on. I even hollered out some techniques I thought ought to be tried, and every one was. By the time they were half-way through, she was dead behind her eyes." Preston paused and looked away. "Then I'm being lifted out of my chair, laughing and all surprised, and next thing I'm on my back on the table, 'cause I don't perform all that well with no legs and all. Wolf tells her to straddle me, while he's undoing my pants. She gazes at him, and she's a mess, face all bruised and blood trickling out of her nose, and she says no. I don't know how she could have it in her to say no; but she does, and old Wolf slaps her so hard I think her face will come right off her head, and then his knife is at her neck. So she does it finally, and somewhere in there Wolf's attention turns away, and she passes out, just slumps over and falls off the table. No one but me even noticed. It was over for them when they sat her on the cripple."

Dillon said, "Preston . . ."

"You know what I thought about?"

Dillon shook his head.

"Remember Old Lady Crummet's cat? Old Charlie? I thought about old Charlie while I was struggling to get my pants back on up on the pool table. While I should have been thinking how the hell I was going to get down and get more drugs, I was thinking of old Charlie. I was remembering how I told myself, clear back then, if I ever got that far out again—*anytime* in my life—well, that would be the end of me." He nodded, staring at the Luger. "Well, last night I did it." He looked at Dillon straight in the eye as he raised the gun. "I left you a note, Dillon. And I left something else."

He put the gun to his temple; Dillon screamed and lunged for him, but it wasn't even close. He didn't actually see Preston do it, didn't see the blood or the brains or the mess because he jerked his eyes away the moment he saw the pressure of Preston's finger on the trigger. But Dillon heard it. And he saw it in his head.

I can't begin to describe what's gone on inside me since that day, Pres. There are lots of times I want to take the blame. I mean, you said it: If I hadn't been "mirror,

mirror on the wall," constantly serving up the wrong
answer, well, things might have turned out differently for
you. And I was always so goddamn flip about the reasons I
thought Stacy should dump you and pick up on me—way
before you ever got involved with dope and all those bad
actors. But there was certainly never any danger of her
doing it, and I really don't think I ever meant it. Stacy was
hopelessly yours.

There are other times, though, when I'm so mad at you
I want to shove a steel tube down into your grave and pour
raw sewage into it. Where the hell do you get off blaming
me for your size and temperament? And your *choices*, for
Christ's sake. And where do you get off tricking me into
watching you die?

There's a lot to consider. I have never loved and hated
anyone at the same time and so ferociously as I do you for
what you did. My emotions churn inside me like a hurricane,
and when it's at its worst, I can only lay back and let them
take me away.

I miss you, Pres. I don't miss the drugs and the
craziness of the end, but I miss the real you from back
before.

Your brother

CHAPTER 5

Jennifer sat on the edge of her hospital bed, absently fiddling with the electric position controls while she read the Sunday paper and waited for Coach to come pick her up. There had been no word from her parents, which didn't surprise or bother Jennifer in the least, but she was anxious to get out of there and get home. She always preferred to be home ahead of them, like a wolf marking the corners of its territory. It gave her the hint of an illusion of power or of safety. Of course, it was *only* an illusion. Her only chance in her war against her stepfather was always to be there first and always to be prepared. When she was away for long, the sense of urgency would creep into her throat until she feared she would choke on it.

"Renee Halfmoon," a pitiful John Wayne imitation

at the door said, "crawl back into your hole. Jennifer Lawless'll be takin' over in these here parts, thank ya, pilgrim."

Jen smiled and looked up to see Dillon Hemingway peeking around the doorway at her.

"What're you doing here?" she asked. "Another five or ten minutes I'm outta this place."

"Less than that," he said, then slipped back into his fraudulent facsimile of Rich Little doing the Duke. "Ah come to take ya away from all this, ma'am. It's a sorry thing when a heroine the stature of yourself can't find a gown to cover her backside." In his own voice: "If I invite you to the prom, will you wear that?"

Jennifer glanced down to discover the open back on the ridiculous hospital gown had slid around to the side, exposing part of her hip. She fired the sports section at Dillon. "If you invite me to the prom, I'll wear three rolls of adhesive tape. You won't get your hands on anything but money for my dinner."

"Tape scissors," he said, stepping around the doorway and revealing a pair of jeans and a Wenatchee sweatshirt in one hand and Jennifer's underthings in the other. "I'll bring tape scissors." He threw her the jeans and sweatshirt, then turned toward the hall with the rest. "I'll wait out here with these," he said. "Just give me a few minutes. . . ."

"Where'd you get those?"

"Don't you remember?" Dillon asked, feigning affront. "You said it was a night you'd never forget. You said . . ."

"If you're seeing your life pass before your eyes as we speak," Jennifer said, "it's because the Lord knows it will end in three seconds if you don't give me my underwear."

Dillon opened his mouth to speak.

"Before you say one more word," Jen warned.

"Only fooling." Dillon smiled big and threw the sacred garments in Jen's direction, then stood outside the door while she hurriedly put them on.

"Where'd the sweatshirt come from?" she called to him.

"It was from the warrior's room untimely ripped," Dillon called back, bastardizing Shakespeare beyond even his own usual limit. "It's a trophy. Like a ground squirrel's tail or a moose head."

"Where'd it come from?" Jennifer asked again, patiently.

"Renee Halfmoon. She wanted you to have it."

"Really?" Jen said as Dillon walked back into the room, having sensed she was dressed. "Really? It came from Renee Halfmoon?"

"Really."

"God, that's *nice*."

Dillon shook his head. "Chicks," he said. "You guys really know how to compete. If I'd have been Renee Halfmoon and I played as good a game as she played and still lost, I'd have ripped a set of lockers off the wall, or something dignified like that. Renee Halfmoon gives you her sweatshirt. No wonder wars have to be fought by men."

"No wonder at all," Jen said, standing. "Get me out of here."

Outside, Dillon opened the van's passenger door to let Jen in. Jen knew Dillon's brother, Preston, had owned the van—outfitted with state-of-the-art wheelchair gear, including a lift that Preston had seldom used and apparatus to operate the accelerator and brakes by hand—after he was crippled and before he died. Dillon had not altered it since Preston's death and had in fact, because of an oversight on the part of the Department of Licensing, been able to keep the handicapped license plates. It was never hard to find a good parking place.

Jennifer noticed the plates, as she did every time she rode with Dillon, and shook her head disapprovingly. "You could go to hell for that, you know."

"I only keep them for Caldwell."

"Why Caldwell?"

"He called me into his office a couple of months ago to let me know what a slime bucket he thought I was for taking advantage of the less fortunate in our society."

"What did you say?"

"I told him if they could see my golf game, they'd issue me handicapped plates anyway."

Jennifer smiled. "Bet he thought that was cute."

"Not so you'd notice. But it gave him the opening to tell me what a horse's ass I am for withholding my 'marvelous athletic talents' from the school."

"I don't get the connection."

"There isn't one, other than it falls under the general heading of *1001 Ways to Shirk Responsibility*, by John Caldwell as told to Dillon Hemingway." Dillon pulled the van out of the hospital parking lot and eased onto Grande Avenue, headed up onto the North Hill. They rode in silence a few moments, Jen staring out the window at the sledding hill in Chief Joseph Park, lost in thoughts about the game.

"How'd you get my stuff?" she asked, finally.

"I called Coach," Dillon said, "to tell her I'd like to pick you up. She said your sister was there at her place, so I dropped by and picked up the key. Where the hell are your parents?"

Jen shrugged. "Why?"

"If I'd had a game as important as Wenatchee, my dad wouldn't have missed it for anything."

Jen shrugged again. "They're just not into it, that's all. That's okay with me. You know that."

Dillon nodded. He did know that. He just didn't know *why*. After all the intimate conversations, each riding the freeway of that immediate magical connection running between them, he thought he knew her, and yet he knew almost nothing *about* her. "Could I ask you a personal question?"

"You can ask."

"You don't have to answer. . . ."

"I know that."

"How come you wanted your sister to stay at Coach's last night?"

"I didn't know where my parents were."

"But you didn't want Coach to call."

"Like I said"—Jen stared out the window again—"you can ask. . . ."

"It just seemed weird, that's all."

"Almost everything about my parents is weird," Jen said. "I really don't like to talk about them, okay? I made a decision a long time ago that if I pretend they don't exist, I don't have to deal with them."

Dillon pulled into the huge circular driveway in front of Jen's house and set the parking brake. "Want me to come in?" he asked.

"What for?"

"How cordial," he said. "What happened to 'Why, sure, Dillon. I'll make you a nice cup of hot chocolate in gratitude for your braving the cold and snow to bring me home from the hospital when my parents are nowhere to be found'?"

Jennifer snapped to and gave a short laugh. "I'm sorry. Actually I was thinking I'd like to be alone for a little while before my sister gets back and my parents come home. I didn't mean that to be bitchy."

She leaned over and gave him a quick hug. "I'll talk to you later—probably tomorrow at school, okay?"

Dillon drove slowly back down Grande, cutting through the downtown area, then south on Post Street toward his home, wondering what was being left out of Jennifer's story. He felt a lot for her, might even be in love if he could figure out what to do about Stacy Ryder, bouncing around in his brain like the monster within all of us, but something was missing. Part of it was that some of the time she didn't even seem like a girl to him. She was tall and pretty and athletic and all that—all things he found extremely attractive in females—but as often as not there were no sexual considerations. He knew that couldn't be coming from him because he had sexual considerations about *everything*. His sister, Christy, had *stuffed animals* he thought were sexy. So it had to be coming from Jen or *not* coming from Jen. And yet she never pushed him away from her in any kind of way that made him doubt his masculinity or think she was interested in someone else. Since their first meeting at school they had spent a lot of time together, got to know each other through one another's pain, in a fashion—a deep, *risky,* trusting fashion—that Dillon almost *never* allowed, especially with Preston's death so fresh in his experience. But there were areas, specifically those around Jen's family, where she just zoned out on him. He knew everyone had secrets. Hell, he hadn't told her everything about Preston, either, but the only reason not to tell was that it took him to a place within himself that he simply couldn't allow anyone to see, the place where he believed that his very existence might have caused the death of his brother. If the same was true for Jen—if there was something *that* dark— something really crazy must be going on in her family.

Deciding there was no sense worrying about what he couldn't change, he forced his crazy thoughts into the back of his mind and drove on home.

Jennifer watched out the window as her mother and stepfather pulled their new Chrysler New Yorker into the driveway, watched a second to see that her stepdad was sober, and considered going up to her room and pretending she was asleep. She decided against it and settled onto the couch with her lit book, declining to greet them when they came through the door, instead letting them find her.

"Hi, baby," her mom called from the kitchen as she removed her boots. "How was the game? We heard you won. The paper said you got hurt. Are you all right?"

Jen fielded only the last question. "I'm fine," she called back. "Just a bump on the head. They wanted to see if I had a concussion."

"A concussion!" Her mom came into the living room. "You got a concussion?"

Jennifer hated it when her mother feigned concern—especially after the fact. Linda Lawless had shown her colors time and time and time again when it came to choosing between her children and anything else she wanted to do, and as far as Jen could see, the kids had yet to come in first. She understood that, expected no more, but hated it when her mom came up with these feeble gestures which belied the truth and which made it all that much harder to protect her mother when the times came. And the times always came. "It wasn't a concussion," she lied. "They just wanted to be sure."

"So tell me about the game," her mom said.

Jen could hear her stepfather coming into the kitchen from outside. Handing her mother the sports section, she suddenly wished she'd gone to her room. "It's all in there," she said. "They tell it a lot better than I could."

"Are you mad that we didn't go?"

"No," Jen lied again. "I'm not mad. I just don't want to go over it all again, that's all. Listen, I'm kind of tired. I think I'll go up and take a nap."

Her mother hugged Jen's tightening body. "Okay, why don't you say hi to your dad first."

"He's not my dad," Jen said matter-of-factly, in exactly the same tone she used every time her mother called T.B. that.

"T.B., then . . ."

"I'll see him later. I'm going to bed."

She closed the door behind her and locked the dead bolt. It didn't do any good, she had to let him in when he wanted—that was the rule—but again, there was that illusion of safety. Jen was furious at her mother for suggesting she say *anything* to T.B., as if he acted like a real father, as if he weren't given to drunken rages that sent the whole family out into the night desperate for sanctuary. She pictured herself and her sister standing knee-deep in snow in their galoshes and nightgowns, a packed suitcase apiece weighing them down as their mother directed them to keep to the woods, away from the road so he wouldn't spot them. Her mother would exhibit cuts and swelling and usually some blood as she lugged her own suitcase. These were the only times Jennifer saw her mother as strong: when her mom was terrified and angry and physically hurt and immediately fearful that T.B. would indeed someday kill one of them. The first time Jen saw her mother like that, she really believed that they'd all finally get away, that her mother would finally protect them. The sixth or seventh time—she had lost count—she had seen her mother like that, she knew they all were stuck with it forever. T.B. was too smart and too strong, and her mother was far, far too weak. Jen would have escaped with her sister a long time ago, but she really believed—with good reason—that her mother would be killed or injured beyond repair.

Jennifer lay down on her back and pulled the pillow over her eyes, trying to let the tension drain the way

Coach had taught her. Starting at her head, she visualized it running the length of her body until it exited the soles of her feet, all the time breathing deeply, sucking the air clear down into her pelvis.

<<<>>>

T.B. seems different from the other men Mom has brought home since Dad left—or rather, since Mom kicked Dad out, sort of. J. Maddy told on Dad, a couple of years after Grampa died. Without Grampa, Dad's nocturnal visits became unbearable for J. Maddy, and so she finally just told. There had been a filmstrip in her second-grade classroom called *Good Touch, Bad Touch*, and it was pretty clear to J. Maddy that what Dad was doing was definitely "bad touch." In the film they said you weren't supposed to keep that secret—the one about someone touching you bad—that when people told you to keep that secret, it was a trick and you should run and tell your mother, and if she won't listen, tell some other grown-up you trust. J. Maddy doesn't know exactly how it all happened; but she told Mom, and Mom got very angry and said it couldn't be true and that she should never, *never* say anything like that again. So J. Maddy did just what the filmstrip said. She told her teacher. Then a man showed up at school and was nice to her and asked her some easy questions in the principal's office, and when she got home, Dad was gone. Mom was in tears, and she screamed at J. Maddy (whom she refused to call that, even after J. Maddy had requested it at Grampa's funeral) and told her now look what she had done, but the man threatened to take J. Maddy someplace safe if Mom couldn't pull it together. Mom pulled it together, at least until the man left, and then they went to this woman called a therapist so they could talk without Mom yelling, and when that was finally over, Mom was able to tell J. Maddy that she was sorry she hadn't protected her.

That felt really good because it seemed like Mom meant it, and for what seemed like a long time, they got closer and closer, and J. Maddy started to love her mom and maybe even trust her for the first time.

But that turned out to be a trick, too. Mom wasn't really sorry. She couldn't have been because she started bringing mean men home, men who would hit her and hit J. Maddy sometimes, too.

Only one of them ever touched her bad, and she was able to scream and run away, and that scared him off; but the bond that started taking hold during the time right after the therapy started to unravel, and more and more often J. Maddy found herself trying to answer the impossible question "Why are you doing this to me?"

every time something went wrong with her and one of these men.

But now there's T.B. He seems different. He plays with her and buys her things. He almost never gets mad, but you can tell when he does because his face gets really red and it looks like there's a rope under the skin on his neck. He doesn't explode, though; he just holds it in. J. Maddy thinks he's rich because he wears fancy suits and brings presents, and Mom seems happier than she's been in a long time—maybe ever—and for the first time in a long time J. Maddy doesn't feel that she's the reason her mom's life is awful. That feels *wonderful* to J. Maddy. The only person she has to take care of is herself, and that makes her feel *free*. She treats T.B. really well and almost never misbehaves when he comes over because "we don't want to scare him off now, do we?"

J. Maddy agrees. We don't want to scare him off.

«‹›»

Jennifer pulled the pillow harder against her face. *Tricks,* she thought. *Always tricks. The sweeter something looks, the uglier it really is.* And then she slid into thinking something that had been bothering her quite a bit in the past few months. *I'm a trick. Four-point-O average, "incomparable athlete," common sense up the wazoo; all of it a lie. I can't even keep my mother's husband out of my bed. How crazy is that?* She pulled the pillow even tighter against her face, recalling the number of times just this year that she had contemplated suicide. Not just thought about dying, but about how she'd do it.

«‹«‹››»

T.B. comes into the room that first night. An old, uneasy feeling creeps into J. Maddy, but she forces it down, pretending to be asleep. He sits on the side of her bed as she assesses whether there is danger, but T.B. doesn't feel as "creepy" as Dad used to. And J. Maddy is nine now; she feels stronger.

He sits on the side of the bed and puts his hands in the middle of her back as she lies pretending to sleep on her stomach, and he rubs gently. He says, "Jennifer," softly.

Nothing.

"Jennifer."

J. Maddy gives a start, then stretches sleepily. "Huh?"

"Can I talk to you for a minute?"

She turns over, rubbing her eyes. "Sure. What?"

"Your mother wants me to stay here tonight. Is that all right with you?"

"Where is she?"

"She went to the store to get some more beer. She'll

be back in a little while. I just want to make sure it's okay with you, that you're comfortable having me stay with her."

J. Maddy doesn't know what to say, but she's become quite expert at saying whatever will not hurt someone's feelings. Actually she doesn't know whether she cares or not. She knows she likes it better when her mother is happy, and she recognizes that she likes it a lot better when she's not the one who has to make that happen. T.B.'s hand moves to her shoulder, and she freezes. He quickly takes it away.

"It's okay with me," J. Maddy says. "If Mom wants you to."

"Don't tell her I came in to ask, okay, Jen?" T.B. says. "I don't want her to think I have to have your permission, but I know it's tough when your family's been through a divorce sometimes. You don't want someone moving into your dad's spot."

J. Maddy sits up. "My dad didn't have a spot," she says. "He's been gone a long time. He didn't leave a spot. Don't worry about that."

T.B. leans over and kisses her quickly on the cheek. He says, "Remember, no need to tell your mom we had this little talk. It'd just worry her that I worry about your feelings. Okay?"

J. Maddy says okay, not knowing why it doesn't feel quite right, why it reminds her of her dad. It makes sense, though, because T.B. seems nice, and when he's with her mom, she treats J. Maddy better.

Over the next few months T.B. spends a lot more time at their house, and he comes into the room increasingly often, sometimes to read J. Maddy stories and sometimes just to talk, about her day in school or her friends or one of her little projects. She feels more and more comfortable with it, even though he comes in only when her mom has gone somewhere or is taking a bath or down in the basement working on her crafts. T.B. is always interested in what she's doing and doesn't push at all. And he plays ball with her. He sets up a backboard over the garage, buys a really good basketball, and plays H.O.R.S.E. and one-on-one tirelessly.

And then it shifts. Not gradually—though maybe she could have seen it coming if she hadn't wanted to like him so much—but instantaneously.

<<«»>>

Tricks, Jennifer thought. *The better it looks, the uglier it really is.* She brought the pillow down to her chest. When she got into this space, nothing but time could bring her out. She was barely aware of the game the night before, of her athletic heroics or the accolades she received in the morning newspaper. She was only aware that her life was a lie—and that the hopeless road before her stretched out forever. She tried to force thoughts of that first time out of her head, but the reel ran on. . . .

«‹‹›»›

J. Maddy sits at her desk, reading a book about a boy named Chip Hilton, by Clair Bee. It is a book for boys, her mother has told her. Girls aren't supposed to be interested in sports. But T.B. chides her mom gently about old-fashioned thinking and tells J. Maddy about several more books in the Chip Hilton series, all about the same boy, first in high school and then in college, who is a superathlete with a wise father who has died and with a lot of good friends. The books cover his adventures in football, basketball, and baseball, but J. Maddy is interested only in the ones about basketball and has scoured the city library in search of them all. She doesn't care that they are old with faded covers and pages ready to fall out between her fingers like over-boiled chicken off the bone. She loves them for their action and for their endings. The good guys always win, and they win so well that the bad guys realize it and turn good. J. Maddy can completely lose herself in a Chip Hilton story.

She hears his voice behind her and starts a little, though only from surprise. T.B. has J. Maddy's trust now. She is not afraid to let him come into her room.

"Whatcha reading?" he asks, leaning over her shoulder to peek.

She shows him the cover. *Hoop Crazy.*

T.B. nods. "I remember that. It's a good one. How far are you?"

J. Maddy pinches the pages of the first three chapters together between her thumb and forefinger, indicating her progress. If she starts talking, she knows he will stay and she'll have to put the book down.

T.B. says no more, and J. Maddy returns to the book, semi-consciously noting that he hasn't left but is sitting on the bed. She turns uncomfortably, but before she can speak, he motions her to continue reading. "Don't worry about me," he says, "I'm just relaxing. Your mom went to a meeting. She'll be late."

She is suddenly uncomfortable with him sitting there but forces herself to read another page before turning from her desk. Finally she can't stand the silence. "You want to play a game?" she asks. "Monopoly or something?"

T.B. shakes his head and says no. "Go ahead with your book," he says.

J. Maddy goes on, forcing her thoughts away from these strange feelings, familiar feelings. Then his hand is on her shoulder again; only this time it feels different, maybe a little forceful. He massages her neck and runs his hands down her shoulders. J. Maddy shrugs and pulls away. "That tickles," she says, and giggles, though she doesn't really feel like laughing, and he pulls her back, still running his hands over her back, and suddenly all she wants is to get away. "No," she says, and starts to stand, but T.B. pushes her down on the chair, hard.

"Just do what I tell you," he says, "and it won't hurt." His breath smells of alcohol, hot and sweet. His hands slide under her arms and around to her chest, and she pulls violently away; but his fingers are like vises, and he pinches her, hard. J. Maddy shrieks and starts to cry. She calls for her mother, but of course, there's no answer.

J. Maddy's mind races as T.B. carries her to the bed, trying to think what she's learned at school in the *Good Touch, Bad Touch* classes; but the wheels only spin in panic, and she can't concentrate, can't remember. He's undressing her now. Feelings she hasn't felt for years, since her father left, roar into her throat and choke her with terror. T.B. releases her for a second to undo his pants, and she instinctively rolls off the bottom of the bed, hitting the floor on the run, but he is much too quick and kicks his foot against the door as she tries to jerk it open. He slaps her hard across the face, and she drops to the floor in tears as he quickly drags the desk in front of the door. There are no more words; there is no more resistance. J. Maddy does what she learned to do when her father came into her room years ago: She leaves her body there, but she takes her head away. In the distance she hears her sister knocking on the door, but then J. Maddy's gone, picturing clouds and kites and her grandfather. It's harder to stay gone, because T.B. is rough, but she manages out of sheer will, and when he is finished, she lies with her face pressed into the crack between the bed and the wall, no tears, no sound, no feelings.

She hears the desk slide back to its original place, and she hears the door open and close and Dawn's and T.B's voices out in the other room, and that brings her back in a flash. She runs to the door and listens, waiting to hear if he's going after her sister. If he does, she thinks, there's a poker by the fireplace. *I'll get him. I will. I'll get him.*

But the voices are normal. T.B. is saying he doesn't know why Dawn couldn't get the door open or why her sister didn't hear her knocking. He's sorry she was scared. No, she shouldn't go into Jennifer's room. He just checked and Jennifer's asleep.

I'll tell, Jennifer thinks. *Just like before. Wait till I tell Mom. She'll believe me this time, because I proved it before.*

J. Maddy steals across the hall to the bathroom. Locking the door quickly behind her, she strips her pajamas off and steps into the shower. She makes the water as hot as she can stand and washes herself over and over and over again, and though her mind knows she's clean, the icky feeling inside won't go away. She stays until the water begins to turn cold, carefully touching her private parts with the washcloth. There is blood, and it hurts terribly. Just wait, she'll tell.

She lies in her bed with the light on, trying to read her book, waiting; but Mom doesn't come, and it's very late and J. Maddy finally tries to sleep. She can't keep the thoughts out, it's been so long, and she's out of practice—she really thought she was safe with T.B.—and her body begins to convulse, and the convulsions finally give way to sobs, and she cries until she's empty, until she approaches an uneasy sleep. But her dreams immediately wrench her awake, and she lies in the darkness of the room, feeling terrified and invaded and utterly powerless. She wishes she could just die.

The door opens quietly, and J. Maddy hears soft footsteps. Closing her eyes and pulling the covers tight against her chin, she rolls over again into the crack between the bed and the wall. The lamp beside her bed is switched on, and she feels the pressure of someone sitting next to her.

"Jennifer, I have something you need to see." It's T.B.

J. Maddy doesn't move.

"Did you know Rolex almost got run over today?" he says.

Rolex is J. Maddy's and Dawn's dog, a puppy actually. They've had him only three months. He's a golden retriever, and J. Maddy named him Rolex because her mother said he might be a good watchdog. J. Maddy is a whiz at puns. Rolex is also the name of T.B.'s watch.

J. Maddy turns over. She is defiant, eyes blazing, the covers still pulled tight.

"It was close," T.B. says. "Rolex is a very lucky dog. I saved him just in time." He hands J. Maddy a Polaroid picture of her puppy, his head jammed under the back tire of the car, a boot against his neck. His leash is chained to the back bumper.

The boot is T.B.'s.

"I saved him just in time," T.B. says again.

J. Maddy's eyes grow huge as she realizes what this means, and T.B. holds the picture just out of her reach. She looks at him in astonishment, then back at the picture.

"If you tell anyone—*anyone*—what happened in here tonight, I won't be able to get to Rolex in time next time. Do you understand?"

J. Maddy nods quickly. "I won't tell," she says breathlessly. "I promise. I won't tell."

"I believe you, Jennifer. I really do. But you should know that's just the start. If you change your mind and decide to tell anyway, Rolex won't be the only one. I'll get Dawn, and then I'll get your mom. And then I'll get away." He reaches over and places his hands tightly on her cheeks, forcing her to look into his eyes. "I've done it before," he says softly, and J. Maddy is chilled to her marrow.

«« » »

That is the face Jennifer remembered as she clutched tight to the pillow in her room. He came again, of course. As often as twice a week sometimes. It had been less lately, probably in the past year or so, but Jennifer only feared that meant Dawn was next. There was no peace. She had perfected the art of "leaving" when he came in and had perfected the lie in the rest of her life so well that sometimes she forgot how she was trapped. Basketball helped with that. So did her studies. It wasn't hard to be perfect, she thought, when it kept your mind away from such horror. Only during times like these, when she was weakened in some way, did she feel this horrible, empty hopelessness. She would wait it out. She always had.

CHAPTER 6

Dear Preston,

That's what it is, things get misnamed. Stacy said that. Today Mr. Caldwell told me I didn't have any respect. What he meant was, I'm not afraid of him. Mr. Caldwell calls fear respect. That's really not a bad trick if you can get the right people to buy it. See, respect is a good thing, at least the way most people see it. Fear is a bad thing, but it's a lot easier to create. So if you're lazy, or dumb, and don't want to go through what you have to for respect, your next best option is to call something else by its name, like fear. It's like fool's gold. Fear is fool's respect.

The Nobel Prize for that little theory was a three-day vacation, do not pass Go, do not collect your lunch ticket. The rebellious part of you would love me these days, Pres. I spend more time out of school than in, and my grades are still the same. 'Course, part of the reason he booted me might be traced to my delivery. I wasn't exactly scholarly in my presentation. I just needed to get that turdburger out of my face. God, he always catches me in the hall or the lunchroom or someplace where I've just fallen in lust with some girl to hold me over until I can figure out what I'm supposed to do with Jen and Stacy. Then he just pushes until I fight back, which is usually within the first fifteen seconds. The way I normally fight back is to say something about either his bald head or his mother. Neither of us likes to lose face, though he has more to lose—his goes all the way to the back of his head—so we get locked in and end up in a tug-of-war that he always wins because he has been granted the divine gift of suspension.

Yesterday we were in second lunch, with a considerable audience. Pretty soon, nothing short of one of us falling to his knees to beg forgiveness would stop us once we got right down to pretty unpleasant pleasantries. Actually I think I may have wanted the vacation because I had several chances to walk away and didn't.

You were right, Pres. Caldwell got to be an administrator the only way you can if your IQ is roughly equal to the daily average mean temperature from late October through early March—above the forty-fifth parallel. He was a coach. As far as I'm concerned, coaches fall into two categories:

those I like and those I don't. Caldwell is president and lifelong board chair of those I don't, and in fact, he's one of the main reasons I never went out for anything. He and his followers—and they are legion—have somehow confused athletic commitment with patriotism and human spiritual values, among other things. They believe that the way to keep your body and soul free of the Communist plague is to exercise both daily in the athletic arena—the *American* athletic arena—and they also believe Jesus Christ was the best darned quarterback/power forward/third baseman (pick one, depending on your sport of preference) who ever lived, and to tell you the truth, I get tired of them using such a heroic dude as Jesus must have been for such cheap purposes. And when I get *really* tired of it, I usually get time off for bad behavior. I never give him enough to expel me because I know I need an honorable discharge from this place, but I like to think of myself as a chigger in his undershorts. I don't want to make his life a living hell, but I sure want to make it uncomfortable. Yesterday, though, things went a little far.

It started innocently enough. He hollered my last name as I was carrying my tray toward a table.

I said, "Yeah?"

"You given any consideration about what we talked about?"

I love to string him out. "Which thing?" I asked.

"About your turning out for track this spring."

"Yes, sir," I said, "I did," and I continued on toward the table.

"Well?"

"Well, what?"

"What did you decide?"

I said, "I decided not to," and went on to set the tray down beside Jen's.

His standard exasperation with me was about at his chest, working its way quickly toward his throat, at which time I expected his speech to get a little constricted. He took a deep breath. Our wars are famous by now, so the two tables around us grew quiet. "Did you talk with Coach?" he asked.

"No, sir, I didn't."

"I thought we'd agreed you'd talk with Coach before you made your decision."

"No, sir, actually we didn't agree. You said I should, and I said I'd think about it. I thought about it and decided I didn't want to."

A knot about half the size of a seedless grape appeared at his tightening jaw. I wonder how he does that. "You know, Hemingway, you could use a little lesson in respect."

I looked at the floor.

"When are you gonna quit taking from this school, Hemingway? When are you gonna give something back?" By now the quiet had spread to most of the tables in that section of the cafeteria and kids were moving in from outlying areas. "You have athletic talents some of these kids would kill for," he said. "But you don't have enough respect for your school, or your peers, or me to use them for some good."

Now there's a time in these discussions Caldwell and I have semiregularly when I try to reason with him—you know, tell him why *really* I choose to do what I do. That usually comes right before I start talking about his ancestry.

"I do use them for some good, sir. I do triathlons." That really gets up his nose, and I knew it because triathlons are done completely away from school and he's seen my times—broken down into the swimming, running, and cycling components—enough to know that if I'd turn out for the distances in track, I could do some serious ass kicking in the name of Chief Joseph High School. He hates that I choose to do it in the name of Dillon Hemingway.

"That's pretty selfish, don't you think?" he said, loosening his tie a little.

I nodded. "Pretty selfish," I said.

"So you think it's okay to just take what you want from

this place without giving it anything back in return, is that right?"

I felt myself drop a level. I can act pretty cool up to a point, but I don't really like that much of an audience, and since you said some of the things you said about me the day you killed yourself, I do think there are times when I consider myself pretty selfish, and even though I may not do anything about it, I'm not proud of it. So I was quiet.

And Caldwell can *smell* a cornered animal.

"You know, Hemingway, I don't think it's just this school you don't have any respect for. I don't think you have much respect for *anything*. Your dad must feel pretty hopeless, what with all he's been through these last couple of years."

Inside me, I knew he was walking on thin ice because he was into my family now, and if his next move was to bring you into it, he was looking for some serious escalation.

"Mr. Caldwell," I said, and by now we had the full cafeteria hanging on our every word, "I don't mind you harassing me in the name of respect and school spirit and all that. But you want to think twice before you start in on my family." I walked a couple of steps toward him. "You keep saying I don't give anything back to this school. I haven't gotten a grade lower than a B plus since I set foot in this place, and there have been damn few of those. I work my ass off in classes, and I do a pretty good job as trainer for Coach Sherman. Now, my dad pays taxes just like everyone else's folks, so I figure my educational debt is covered. The trouble is, you think a full-service educational system consists of state championships in every sport and if somebody happens to *learn* something along the way, well, that's cool."

"Hemingway," he said, "you're about to get yourself into a lot of trouble. I won't be talked to that way."

I put up my hands. "Fine. I'll go eat my lunch, and you go do whatever it is you do, and we'll forget all about this little chat."

He shook his head. "What're we going to do with you?" he said. "You're going to turn out just like your brother."

He had to do it, Pres. I can be as mad at you as I want, but that is not a consideration I extend to others. I whirled and walked toward him, not really knowing whether I'd take a shot at laying him out or what. "My brother's dead, you flaming asshole. We're all gonna turn out like my brother. You keep it up, though, and you're gonna turn up there sooner."

Caldwell had never seen me go quite that far, and I could see real fear in his eyes. You know how big he is, and he's still in pretty good shape—really good shape, if you want to know—so I don't think he was afraid for his physical self, but he was sure afraid of how far he might have to go to stop me. He was caught, though, just like I was, and he had to play it out.

"Are you threatening me?" he said, holding his ground.

I stopped right in front of him and nodded. "Yup," I said. "I sure am."

"You're out of here, Hemingway. Three days. You're lucky it's not longer."

"And you're lucky I need the time to finish a term paper," I said. "Because I'm going to take the vacation and cut everyone's losses. I'm not going to register a formal complaint with the school board, and I'm not going to see my old man's lawyer." I turned to walk out, then turned back and pointed a shaky finger at him. "But I will next time."

He stood quietly and watched me leave. My temper leaves almost as fast as it comes up, so by the time I got to the door I felt under control, and I wanted a parting shot. "Must have had you worried a minute there, sir," I said with a grin, and patted the top of my head. "It's raining all over your crystal ball."

And speaking of things misnamed, well, strange things abound at Stacy's, some of them things you know about. I didn't have anything to do today—someday Caldwell's got to figure out Dad doesn't ground me or give me eight million menial jobs to do so I won't learn the wrong lesson from being laid off from my job at the Learning Factory—so I went over to Stacy's house to pass some time. It seems she and I have had a real unpredictable relationship ever since you left. Sometimes we're closer than Siamese twins joined at the heart, and sometimes we're so distant from one another we seem to live in different times; and I never know how it's going to be from day to day. She left for about six months shortly after your funeral, to stay with some relatives in South Dakota; her parents said she needed to heal. I was really hurt because she was gone a week before I even knew she left, and I never did hear it from her. I heard it from her parents. It took Stace and me a little while to clear that up when she got back because I was pretty pissy, but we finally did okay, I think.

Then, about four months later, her parents adopted a baby. She said one of her cousins in South Dakota got pregnant and no one there felt like they could keep it, so Mr. and Mrs. Ryder came to the rescue even though they're fairly old and felt like they'd put in their time raising their family. I heard them say that a million times when they were crying the Winnebago Blues, which is what I call the sad song they sing about having to send Stacy to college rather than throwing everything into a brand-new Winnebago and heading out to see the continent. Neither of them has retired yet, though Mr. Ryder only works part-time now and plans to quit altogether at the end of this year and Mrs. Ryder says she can quit her law practice anytime they decide to take off. Anyway, since Stacy's been back, she's spent a fair amount of time absent from school, taking care of her new brother. I knew she'd be there today because she always misses Fridays.

When I showed up at the door, she said, "Hi. Got another vacation, huh? What'd you say this time?"

"I don't think it was what I said. I think it was how I said it."

She nodded. "My best guess is that it was both. How long you out for?"

I said, "Three days."

"That's not bad. Wanna do something? I'm *bored*. Taking care of a kid ain't all it's cracked up to be."

"Yeah," I said. "I do wanna do something. But what *about* the kid? You gonna leave him here to take care of himself?"

"No," she said. "I'm going to take him with us. We can just put him in the car seat and pack his duds and go wherever we want. He needs to learn to travel. He may be a Winnebago baby by this time next year, to hear my parents talk." She packed what looked to me to be a week's supply of those paper diapers, stuffed several bottles into a large cloth bag, dragged the car seat out of the back room, and handed it to me as she opened the kitchen door leading out to your van. There had to be three feet of snow on the ground, and the temperature had been stuck down below zero somewhere for the past three days, but old Ryan—that's this Ryder's name—was bundled up like a miniature Michelin tire baby and no cold got on his brand-new powdered butt.

"So how are your parents liking second parenthood?" I asked as we pulled into McDonald's to get a little breakfast before chauffeuring young Ryan Ryder on his first trek out into the snowy wilderness.

"I think they're liking it okay," she said. "Actually I take care of him quite a bit. I was the one who really pushed to take him when my cousin was talking about putting him up for adoption, so I figure I have to help out as much as I can."

"Boy, I know," I said. "I haven't seen a whole lot of you since you came back."

She said, "Kids take a lot of work."

"How old are your parents?" I asked.

"They're both sixty-one," she said.

You know what that means, Pres? That means they'll be almost eighty when this little boogernose is ready to go out and take on the world. I thought that, but I didn't say it. Stacy has always been a mind reader, though. She said,

"Ronald Reagan was over eighty when he finished his presidency."

"And wasn't he a prize," I said.

She said, "I get your point, but like I said, a lot of it will fall to me."

Ryan's contribution to the conversation was to sit in the back working on the release buttons to the car seat, babbling unintelligible syllables and drooling at a rate that made me think there must be a fire in his lap.

"That's like being a parent yourself, though, really," I said. "I mean, you still going to school and everything? College, I mean."

"I'll make it," she said. "People do it all the time."

"Yeah, but they don't always do it well."

Stacy got quiet all of a sudden and just looked out her window. Finally she turned to me and said, "Look, Dillon, I've got all kinds of people to tell me not to have anything to do with this, okay? I'm hoping you won't turn out to be one of them. What I would like to do today is ride in your van with you and the munchkin and not hear any negative words about anything and just make contact with you again. Do you think that would be possible?"

"Not another negative word will race past my voice box and out my lips," I said. "We'll just be a lovely young couple out with their child, enjoying the winter wonderland."

She nodded. "Thank you."

We drove along in silence for a bit, Stacy turned around halfway in the van seat, letting Ryan play with her finger, as I guided the van through the switchbacks that lead up to the top of Mount Spokane, where we could watch people ski and look about halfway around the world in any direction. Remember when Mom and Dad used to take us up there for picnics in the summer? God, I thought it really was the top of the world. You used to tell me it was lame as *real* mountains go, but it sure seemed like a major peak to me.

As we neared the top, I glanced into the rearview mirror to see Ryan had been rocked to sleep by my driving. Out of the corner of my eye I could see Stacy just staring at him. I couldn't read her thoughts, couldn't even guess, really, but it was a look I hadn't seen on her.

"What's going to happen to us, Stace?" I asked by way of "making contact again."

"What do you mean?"

"I don't know exactly. I mean, I've been in love with you all my life while you were in love with my brother. We both watched him botch his life beyond belief while I kept mine in pretty good shape, all things considered, but nothing changed with the three of us. I was your friend, and he was your honey. Now he's dead, by his own doing." I shook my head and stared out the windshield a minute, trying to arrange it in my head so it would make better sense coming out of my mouth, to no avail.

"I used to think as long as he was alive—with no idea that he ever wouldn't be—that I didn't have a chance with you. Then he died, and I realized as long as he's dead, I don't have a chance with you."

She looked over and smiled, nodding, almost sadly, I thought, but not negating any of my words. I didn't expect her to. I wasn't fishing; I was telling it the way I knew it to be. "What do you want me to say?" she asked.

"Something that helps it all make sense," I said.

"What about the girl you've been spending time with? The basketball chick."

"Jen?"

"Yeah."

"What about her?"

"How come you guys don't get something going? You spend enough time together."

I wanted to be honest, Pres. Maybe that's why I'm telling you all of this, even though it embarrasses me to let you know how I talk about you, but I'm so goddamn tired of being confused and not knowing which of my passions to take where. Stacy has always been a good clearinghouse for me, even when you were alive and I ate my heart out sometimes, wanting her to dump you for me, but she was still a better friend than anything. "I don't know, Stace," I said. "I don't know whether it's her or me. Something in me is more drawn to her than anyone or anything since you, but we don't click as partners: you know, boyfriends and girlfriends, that kind of stuff. You know how sometimes you can't imagine being physical with someone?"

"You mean sexual?" Of course, she knew that. It was the perfect description of me for her. She nodded.

"It's like that. I don't get it. I mean, sometimes I actually feel like I love her, it's that intense. But it just doesn't fit anything that I know about love."

I pulled into the parking lot at the bottom of the ski hill and stepped down on the parking brake, leaving the van running for heat. Ryan woke when the driving motion stopped and immediately started crying. Stacy reached back and unhooked the latches on the car seat, setting him free to be brought into her lap. She dug down into the bag and pulled out a bottle, twisting the lid slightly to let a little air in, and stuck the nipple in his mouth. He was instantly at peace with his world. You should see her with that kid, Pres. Like it's meant to be.

"You don't know anything about love," Stacy said. "Neither do I. Probably neither does Jen. Don't feel bad, though. Our parents don't either." She looked out the side window. "There are so many crazy things, dangerous things sometimes, that we're taught to call love. . . ." Her voice trailed off. The strain in it made me ache. She turned back and looked me straight in the eye. "There are too many tricks, Dillon. Too many tricks," and I remembered hearing Jen say almost those exact words. "Things have the wrong names. Remember that time a long time ago when I showed you those Chinese handcuffs? At that carnival? I got them from this gypsy lady. She told me they were a secret of life; I remember that. I thought she was full of shit, but you know, she might have been right. When you're a kid, you think you can pull hard enough to get them off, but Arnold Schwarzenegger couldn't get those things off his fingers. You have to do exactly the opposite what it seems you should do. You have to let go. Remember the first time your dad tried to teach you to drive on ice? How when the car started to slide you had to turn *into* the slide while every nerve in your body said to turn the other way? I think life is like that a lot, way more than we know. And I think *love* is particularly like that. We think we're supposed to *fight* for it when we're really supposed to let go; you know, turn *into* it."

Ryan stirred in her lap. He had fallen asleep, and the bottle lay between his legs. Stacy picked it up and handed it back. The nipple slid in like it was custom made for his mouth. Something in his face gave me a powerful rush of déjà vu, but it passed in a heartbeat.

"We get crazy when we can't make things be like the world tells us they are." She looked back out the window. "It was that way for me and your brother, I think. I mean, how could I have loved him that last year? I didn't even know who he was. He was way more attracted to drugs and bikers and that whole lifestyle than he was to me. But somebody told me that if you really loved somebody, you stayed with him no matter what. You had to *fight* for him." She laughed. "Hell, I was convinced."

I knew she was right, but it wasn't helping. I remember the day you died, when we were at Jackie's, having breakfast, and you talked about how you had really screwed things up with her. You thought you were thinking it, but you were really saying it out loud. But I really struggled with what she was saying because I couldn't let her go—didn't know how—and I had no idea *what* I'd have to let go of to get my mind straight about Jen.

Stacy bundled Ryan up, and we walked into the lodge for a cup of hot chocolate. There weren't many skiers, its being a weekday and all, but the view from the tables inside faces the hill directly, and you get a great view of the few diehards who were there. Ryan was awake now, babbling on and checking out gravity with a spoon that Stacy kept picking up and handing back to him. She has a lot of patience. I think you need that with a kid.

Then she asked me if I'd ever seen a marriage I wanted to have.

"What do you mean?"

"Exactly that. Who do you know that has a marriage that you want yours to be like?"

I thought a minute. No surprise to you that my mind didn't go directly to Mom and Dad. The only one that came to mind was her folks', so I said that.

She laughed. "That the best you can do? My parents have stayed together because they ignore each other about eighty-five percent of the time. They even have their sleep schedules set up so one is awake when the other isn't. They'd be a perfect couple to man the distant early warning system."

I was surprised. "Really? I always thought they got along really well."

"They do get along really well. They never talk about anything they can fight about. If my parents' life were a food, it would be soggy rice cakes."

"Well, there have to be *some* good ones."

She shrugged. "Show me."

I couldn't. I couldn't think of *one*, Pres, so I just sat there, taking over the spoon-retrieving duty while Stacy stared out the window at the mountain. I couldn't figure out what had changed, or why. Stacy used to be so *up*. She was the one we could always count on to see the one marshmallow in the sump. Your death had been hard on her, really hard. But that was two years ago, and if Stacy is anything, she's resilient.

I handed Ryan the spoon, and he held it tight, his eyes locked on mine. He smiled big and dropped it once again to the floor. I felt I was in obedience school.

When I got home tonight, I figured it all out. You must have been laughing your ass off reading the first part of this. What a frigging genius I turned out to be. I was sitting on the edge of my bed getting ready to write this, thinking of maybe signing up for the track team at school so I could quit before the first practice and drive Mr. Caldwell a little farther up the wall when a picture completely filled my head. It was a picture—a real picture—in a family album. Our family album, Pres. It was Ryan holding the spoon, smiling big as all outdoors, getting ready to drop that sucker right on its spoony head. Only the picture was sixteen years old at least. I dug through the albums Mom kept when she was still here, half wondering why she hadn't taken them with her—hell, she was the only one who ever looked at them—and I found the one with my name on it and flipped it open to the second page—right where I knew it would be. The background was different. We weren't on Mount Spokane;

we were at that little hamburger place that used to be around the corner from our house, Fat Albert's, I think it was called. I was about one—the back of the picture said a year and a month—sitting with a spoon poised to drop through the bomb bay doors and a big shit-eating grin on my face. Ryan's grin.

So that's it. The plot thickens. I *knew* there was no good reason in the world for Stacy's parents to adopt a kid when they were a short dropkick away from being set free. Old Ryan is up to his chubby cheeks in my genes; only they didn't come from me.

I turned out the light and lay back on the pillow, with not the slightest idea how to greet this incontrovertible news and I heard your voice, Pres, clear as a bell. ". . . and I left something else. . . ."

Sweet Jesus.
Your brother

CHAPTER 7

John Caldwell walked through the door to the faculty lounge and directly to the coffeepot, where he inserted a dime into the Styrofoam cup marked "Donations" and poured himself a cup of "hot java," words he mumbled to the collective faculty's growing irritation, *every*time he poured himself coffee. He was agitated and poured the cup too full. "Damn," he whispered as it burned his lip and splashed down over the front of his white shirt. Don Morgan, a social studies teacher and boys' JV baseball coach, looked up and smiled. "Tough day, Chief?"

"Tough day," Caldwell said back. "You know, I do my best to understand these kids, but sometimes it just baffles me." His eyes went to the door, and beyond, and he said to himself, "Just baffles me."

"Who's baffling today?" Morgan asked. "Someone

in particular or just kids in general?" It was the general faculty opinion that Caldwell wasn't all that smart and was probably a little hyperactive and out of control sometimes, but he was liked because he worked hard at his job and really wanted to do it right. The fact that he overshot his boundaries fairly regularly with the kids was forgivable because he kept a reasonably heavy disciplinary hand, making everyone's job a little easier. And he always supported the staff in *any* conflict with a student.

"It's that damned Hemingway," Caldwell said.

"Three days go fast."

"Too fast. Today's his first day back. And you know how he shows up?" Caldwell shook his head in genuine disbelief. "You know how he shows up?"

Morgan did know how he had shown up because Dillon was in his morning U.S. government class. Dillon had hustled through the door about two minutes late, scurrying down the aisle to his customary front-row seat, whispering, "Sorry I'm late, sir, I got held up in English."

"Didn't by any chance have something to do with your T-shirt," Morgan had said.

Dillon had looked down, reading his T-shirt silently upside down, then looked back up in perfect innocence. "No, sir. It's grammatically correct."

The T-shirt read, in giant black letters:

GIVE A PERSON GUTS
AND
SHIT'LL DO FOR BRAINS

It was the same shirt Dillon wore each time he competed in a triathlon, a slogan that made a lot of sense, given the grueling physical nature of the activity.

"No," Morgan lied, "how does he show up?"

"In a goddamn pornographic T-shirt," Caldwell said, shaking his head. "I send him out of here because he can't seem to show respect for anything or anyone, and his first day back he shows up in a pornographic T-shirt. What do you do about a kid who just won't learn?"

Kathy Sherman walked into the room from her first PE class, poured herself a cup of coffee, and plopped down on the couch with the morning paper.

Morgan looked back down at his papers. "Stop trying to teach him, I guess," he said. "What are you going to do?"

"I'm not sure. This is a tough kid," Caldwell said.

Kathy looked up from her paper. "You talking about Dillon?"

Caldwell was reluctant to say. Kathy Sherman had a reputation for standing up for the students in certain situations; that was fine with Caldwell as long as it wasn't in preference to staff or administration. She had embarrassed him on more than one occasion with questions that seemed to set him up in front of the troops. He hated that, but he was always gracious. Because you had to be, really, when you got shown up so often. Graciousness was a basic survival tactic for John Caldwell. Secretly, though, he hated her. He hated that she was by far the most successful coach in town—probably in the state—and that she accomplished that without the win-at-all-costs philosophy he considered so important in sports, and in life for that matter. She was always giving her kids a *voice* as she called it, and that just didn't make sense. And she liked Dillon Hemingway, the biggest waste since New York's floating, homeless garbage barge. Besides, he thought she must be gay. Actually, he *hoped* she was gay because that would explain a lot of things, though he had no idea how. The fact that she had been married for several years and was now often in the company of a local TV newscaster didn't sway his suspicion one iota because it was a well-known John Caldwell policy to figure out how he wanted things to be, then the facts be damned.

Morgan answered Kathy's question for him. "Yeah, we're talking about Dillon."

"Must've seen his shirt, huh?" Kathy smiled.

"I suppose you think that's acceptable," Caldwell said, setting his cup aside and leaning forward, ready for battle.

Kathy shrugged. "I don't know. I mean, *I* wouldn't wear it."

"I would hope not," Caldwell said, sitting back. "It's just one more—"

"Jennifer Lawless has one like it she wears to practice sometimes, though," Kathy broke in. "I must say, it fits with her outlook about the same way it does with Dillon's."

"You let her wear it to practice?" Caldwell asked incredulously.

"She didn't ask me," Kathy said, turning back to her paper.

"What's the matter with you? Doesn't anyone have any sense of morality or right and wrong anymore? That shirt is *pornographic*. It has the word *shit* right on it." Caldwell was visibly angry.

Kathy put down the paper and pushed her glasses up on her nose. Very quietly she said, "John, you know, you could be a pretty good principal if you could just learn where to make your stands."

Caldwell was blank.

"I'll bet half the kids in school agree with you about

Dillon Hemingway: that he's a smartass and he should use his talents for the good of the school. I've heard several kids say they agree with a lot of what you said to him in the lunchroom the other day. But you blew it picking that place, and you blew it when you brought his brother into it. When you do things like that, everyone automatically thinks you're a jerk."

"His brother was on drugs. He was a dopehead," Caldwell said.

"You think Dillon doesn't know that? You think every kid in this school doesn't know that? John, in the past three years we've had two suicides at this school, aside from Preston Hemingway's. Every kid here was touched by them in some way. Terrified by them. That's a *tender* spot. You don't just gouge it out with a screwdriver. You have to be careful of things like that."

Caldwell's defenses were clogging his throat and his mind. "They're just kids," he said. "They don't understand death."

"Don't *be* a jerk," Kathy said. "They sure as hell understand when something's *gone.*"

Caldwell opened his mouth to continue his argument, then threw up his hands. "That's easy enough for you, Coach," he said instead. "You're a teacher. It looks a little different when you have to run things. *You* didn't have to handle it when all those bikers came after him last year. And neither did *he*. Hell, he was in *your* room using *your* shower so he could go out and be a big triathlon hero. Somebody could have gotten hurt that day. And hurt badly."

"I know it's different being a principal from being a teacher, John. But a power struggle is a power struggle no matter where you run it from. And I don't know one of us that's ever won one." She flipped the newspaper onto the coffee table. "You can go to war over Dillon Hemingway's T-shirt if you want to, but you'll only come out looking bad."

By the time second lunch rolled around, Dillon had pulled the flannel shirt he carried in his book pack on over the offending article of clothing and stood before his locker, talking to Jennifer Lawless, looking for all the world like any all-American student in need of a haircut.

"I thought you'd be out of here again by now," Jen said, opening the top button of his shirt to see the slogan.

"Naw," Dillon answered. "I just wanted to get his circulation going a little, that's all. I'm going to try to stay in at least until B-ball season is over. Last I heard, Caldwell has decided if I'm suspended from school, I'm suspended from my trainer's job, too. Coach asked me to straighten up for a while at least." He reached up and felt his right earlobe. "Soon as the season's over, I think I'll get an earring. That'll give Caldwell something to do till graduation."

Jen smiled. "You know, he really doesn't need you to make him look like an asshole. He does fine by himself."

"I know, I just like to think of myself as one of those yellow highlighters. You know, someone who brings out the prominent characteristics in someone. Listen, do you want to go on a date?"

Jen was off guard. "With who?"

"With *me*, you jerk. What do you mean, 'with who'? You think I'm going to come up and ask you out for someone else?"

Jennifer's reaction was far more intense than seemed warranted. Claustrophobic feelings whirled around her stomach. She was expert at hiding them, and she did; but immense disappointment accompanied them. Dillon Hemingway was the one person around whom she felt comfortable. Their relationship was simple, and she liked that more than anything. "You might," she said, holding a playful facade. "If the price were right."

Dillon ignored that. "Well?"

"I don't know, let me think about it."

He nodded. "Okay. How long do you need? I'm not

real good at waiting when my self-esteem hangs in the balance."

"We can talk about it tomorrow. It's not about you. I'm just really busy, you know. With basketball and everything."

"I know," he said. "I'm not talking about anything elaborate, maybe go someplace nice for dinner."

"We'll talk about it, okay? Meanwhile, you keep yourself in school. I'm *sure* not going out with any dropout."

Dillon stuffed his books into his locker and headed for the parking lot. He figured he had pushed Caldwell a little far with the T-shirt and there was no sense making a target of himself in the lunchroom. Contrary to popular belief, he had *some* limits.

At the door he met Coach Sherman coming in from the gymnasium. She looked at his chest, obviously glad to see he had decided not to push the T-shirt any further. "A word to the wise?" she said.

Dillon smiled. "No one wise in here," he said, tapping his forehead.

She laughed and said, "No one *in* there. If he comes back, tell him to remember to play it cool. I need his athletic medical expertise at State, and Caldwell has just reminded himself of the Day the Warlocks Came."

Dillon grimaced, then shook his head. "Think I'll ever live that down?"

"Nope. It wasn't your finest hour."

"The *idea* was good."

"The idea was bad."

<<«»>>

The funeral is over, and Dillon moves slowly up the church aisle with his parents. His chest is filled with so much pain and confusion and anger he wants to scream, *needs* to scream. But he appears calm because his job is to get his parents—one on each arm, and of *no* help to each other—to the car, which stands waiting only a few yards from the church entrance. It might as well be ten miles. This is the last time he'll ever see them together. Christy trails a few steps behind, silent and removed. This is the conclusion to the family unraveling that began when Preston started to go off the deep end two years ago. At the urging of school counselors they had gone into family therapy clear back then to try to get at the root of Preston's feelings of isolation, of disenfranchisement, but each session brought more and more bogeymen out of the Hemingway closet until no one could figure out how his mom and dad had gotten together in the first place. It seemed there could be no repair. They had stopped the sessions when it seemed the only answer was divorce, and though his parents *didn't* divorce, they might as well have. They stopped talking to each other almost completely, becoming simply two human beings living under one roof, sharing expenses and three children, then finally split up.

Caulder Hemingway's legs fold twice before Dillon can get him to the car, where his dad collapses into the back seat, sobbing inconsolably. His mother, Annie, dry-eyed and staring straight ahead, slides behind the wheel, cold and erect, a steel spear driven deep into the soil, impassively facing the winds of horrible change. Christy stands before both open doors, unable to decide which to enter, which parent to try to touch. Dillon puts his hand in the middle of Christy's back and guides her toward the back, where Christy slides across the seat and buries her head deep into the crook of her dad's arm. She runs her hand carefully down the back of his head, much like a cautious child with a new kitten. Dillon knows he should ride with them, if for no other reason than to save Christy; but he also knows if he doesn't get away, his chest will explode, and like a cornered animal, he sees an escape route and runs.

"I'll bring the van," he says into the window as he shuts the door. His mother nods, and he silently thanks her for not making an issue of it. "I'll see you at home a little later." The long white Chrysler New Yorker pulls slowly away and Dillon turns back toward Preston's van. Remembering the funeral director has informed him Preston's ashes are available at the funeral home when it's convenient for someone to pick them up, Dillon drives the eight short blocks from the church. The door is locked so he rings the bell, stepping in when an attendant opens it. He states his business and is led to a small office in the rear filled with no more than a desk piled high with papers and two chairs. In one of the chairs rests a small plastic box, the name Hemingway tagged across the top in red plastic labeling tape. The attendant asks him to sign two sets of papers and hands him the box. Dillon is surprised at its weight, probably somewhere between six and ten pounds. The residue of a life. He stares at the box as the attendant waits patiently for him to go. She says, "I'm sorry," and Dillon nods, brought back to reality by her words. He finds his way out.

Back in the van, the swarm of feelings in his chest are slowly crowded out by rage, and suddenly all he wants is to get even. He doesn't even know where he'd begin, so he just starts driving, out of town, through Riverside State Park, turning onto every obscure back road that presents itself, in an attempt to become as physically lost as he feels emotionally lost; but that place doesn't exist on this planet, and each back road eventually comes back to pavement. Finally, feeling wholly unsuccessful at any kind of purge, he heads the van back toward town, though the thought of going home brings such emptiness into his heart he has to close off his mind. He thinks that his anger has subsided some and that he can go home and try to help there, at least get Christy out of the center of all that *weight*.

There are only traces of dusk left in the sky as he drives onto Monroe Street toward downtown, passing the Dragon tavern, where Preston used to get his drugs, where the Warlocks hang out. Five or six vintage Harley-Davidson motorcycles lean on their kickstands on the street in front of the bar, and the sight of the bikes brings his rage surging back, swirling into his throat, physically almost choking him. In what will later seem like a timeless blur he slams on the brakes at the next intersection, takes a hard right, and speeds around the block and into the back parking lot of the dry cleaners, housed next door to the Dragon.

He reaches into the rider's seat and picks up the plastic box containing what is left of his brother, snaps the cheap plastic clasp, and opens it. Inside he finds a thick clear plastic bag held closed with a twist tie, exactly like those used to seal Hefty bags. *My brother's in a*

Baggie, he thinks, and almost laughs. *All that's left of my brother is in a goddamn Baggie.* He pulls the bag out of the box, and for a quick second curiosity slips in, leaves him staring at the fine ash, flecked with bone chips and whatever else resisted the heat of the cremator's oven.

Then Dillon ups the ante. He digs into the glove compartment, removes Preston's Luger pistol, tucks it into his belt, fully visible, then stretches around behind the seat to pull up Preston's toolbox, from which he extracts a large flathead screwdriver. With his brother's remains in one hand and the screwdriver in the other, he moves around the side of the Dragon to where the Harleys are parked, pops the locked tanks on all six bikes, and adds a little bit of Preston to each one. Then he walks through the front door of the Dragon, the plastic bag still half full of Preston's ashes and the Luger still tucked in plain sight.

The Dragon is a small tavern, dimly lit by vintage Olympia and Rainier beer signs and shaded overhead lamps hanging at the center of each of three pool tables. Frosted windows prevent outside passersby from seeing in, and the room is ringed by old, hard-seated wooden booths. It's early yet, and the bar is filled to only about a third capacity with bikers and their ladies, and at the moment Dillon walks in, heads turn. He stands before the bar that faces the entrance and waits for quiet. It doesn't take long. He's running on automatic, nearly unaware of the steel grip of fear that waits just beneath his rage.

"My name is Dillon Hemingway," he says in a voice bigger and deeper than he knows. "Some of you guys know me because I used to come in here to drag my brother, Preston, home when he was so messed up he couldn't get to his van. You probably remember Preston as your wienie little crippled gofer, somebody to humiliate when things got slow."

One of the bikers stands up from a booth by the far window. "Hey, you little pimp, what the hell do you want?"

Dillon fingers the gun. "Just a minute of your time," he says, holding up one finger, "just a minute of your time."

"Get the hell out of here," the biker says back.

"I'm almost on my way," Dillon says, glancing around at the rest of the room. "Any of you who can read probably know Preston's dead. He killed himself with the very gun I have tucked here in my belt. He probably had a lot of reasons, but the one that pushed him over the edge was being humiliated beyond endurance right here in this wonderful little yuppie watering hole."

Another of the bikers rises, starts to cross the room, but Dillon says, "I wouldn't do that. You need to know I don't give a shit what happens to me and this gun holds nine very big bullets." He hasn't removed it from his belt yet, but his hand grips the handle. He holds the plastic bag up to eye level. "I brought Preston back with me," he says. "He seemed to like it here a lot, so I thought it might be a good place to leave him."

He opens the bag, holding it in his palm, and begins sprinkling the ashes around. "I'm leaving him here to haunt your asses," he says, taking the gun from his belt. "Anytime something really shitty happens in here—or out there, for that matter—consider that my brother might have had something to do with it. If one of you gets beat up real bad, or a bike goes down, or you lose an old lady, or your kid gets sick and dies, just think about old crippled wienie gofer Preston Hemingway. I got a feeling he's already at work." As he speaks, Dillon spreads the ashes onto the pool tables and the floor and the bar. Several bikers are up; but the gun is out, and no one wants to take the chance. Dillon empties the bag as he backs into the doorway. "Like I said, my name is Dillon Hemingway. I'm in the book, and if you can't read the address, you can find me at Chief Joseph High School. I know what kind of greasy scum you are, and I know you'll come after me, so I want you to know I ain't hiding." In a flash he's out the door, around the corner and starting his van. He expects them to come after him now, but he's out of the parking lot before he sees anyone. It will be later when they discover that Preston Hemingway isn't necessarily a good fuel additive.

«««»»»

The day the Warlocks showed up at Chief Joseph High School was a day when John Caldwell would have been more than willing to turn Dillon Hemingway over to them and call it even. They roared into the parking lot as school was dismissed and 1,722 students between the ages of fourteen and eighteen spilled out onto the campus, headed home. There were at least 55 of the outlaw club's members, and each carried an instrument of considerable weight and substance whose sole purpose for existence was to assist its handler in the destruction of the human skull.

The leader, the huge man known as Wolf, easily six feet five inches tall and a good three hundred pounds, with tattoos covering the length of both arms, stood straddling his chopper. He cupped his hands and boomed, "We wanna talk to Dillon Hemingway! Nobody's lookin' for no trouble. We just want to talk to Dillon Hemingway."

Julie Conners sprinted back inside to the principal's

office, and when she was finally able to spit out what she needed to say, Mr. Caldwell told one of the secretaries to call 911 and got up to go outside. He worked his way through the crowd, which was beginning to lose some of its fear, releasing occasional catcalls to the gang. Pushed to the front of the crowd by his pride and his position, Caldwell stood at the edge of the sidewalk, facing the bikers, and asked them calmly what they wanted.

"We have business with Dillon Hemingway," Wolf repeated.

"I'm sorry," Caldwell said. "We don't have a student here by that name."

"Then how did you know he was a student?" Wolf asked with a sneer. "Maybe he's a teacher or a janitor."

Caldwell stood his ground. "We don't have anyone here by that name."

One of the other bikers yelled, "He *told* us he goes to school here, asshole. Now get him out here before someone gets hurt."

In a lapse of judgment even for him, John Caldwell flared. "You watch your mouth in front of these kids!

The biker laughed. "Yes, *sir.* Try this: he told us he goes to school here, shithead. Now get him out here."

The sounds of sirens broke the gang up, and in seconds the bikers were roaring off in at least five different directions, but not before giving Caldwell a few more titles to try on in front of his students. They also made several pointed comparisons of certain parts of his genitalia to shrunken raisins. He was humiliated and outraged when he stormed into Coach Sherman's office, where Dillon was pulling on his sweats, having spent sixth period—his independent study in PE—swimming a hard two miler.

In the following days Caldwell held Dillon personally responsible for the more than ten thousand dollars in damages brought on by three separate incidents of nocturnal vandalism—as well as for the "image-damaging" television and newspaper coverage—and demanded that Dillon apologize to the student body en masse for bringing Chief Joseph High School into whatever foul dealings he had with a gang of low-life motorcycle bandits.

Afraid he might offend the spiritual sensibilities of many student body members, Dillon never did tell anyone what he had done to bring the gang down on him, rather allowing the popular belief that he had some kind of shady dealings with these people and that he might indeed be, as Caldwell said *many* times to whoever would listen, just like his brother.

CHAPTER 8

Late in the third quarter, while Chief Joseph's girls' basketball team mopped up the floor with crosstown rival David Thompson High, Dillon shoved Kathy McCarty's foot into a bucket of ice to stop the swelling in her ankle, sprained coming down from her fifteenth rebound of the night. Kathy played second string to Jennifer Lawless, who had been on the bench since two minutes into the half because of the lopsided score. Jennifer would get maybe four or five minutes' more playing time before game's end just to keep her loose, but the outcome was not in question—had not been since the first two minutes—and the pressure was off. This was the last league game before the district tournament, due to start in four days out at the community college, and Coach Sherman wanted to be sure her starters were as healthy as possible. She would spend the duration of this game watching girls with less experience to determine who could come off the bench to fill key roles when needed during the tournament.

Jennifer had reluctantly agreed to go on a "date" with Dillon after the game if he would promise not to call it that, and Dillon found himself thinking more about that than his treatment of Kathy McCarty's ankle, though by now sprains were second nature and Kathy was in no danger of losing her foot to malpractice. He had felt an awkwardness with Jen since she agreed to go, and though there was no way he could explain it to himself or anyone else, part of him wished he'd never asked.

Jen was also having difficulty concentrating on the game. She had agreed to the date with Dillon because she felt that if she were ever going to take head-on what appeared to be almost a phobia about boys, Dillon would be the one with whom to do it. He was gentle and respectful with her, and most of the time it was as if neither of them considered that they were of the opposite sex. But Dillon or no Dillon, Jennifer knew how she felt anytime a boy tried to touch her in any kind of sexual way. And she knew why. She remembered how she froze inside and how quickly she rose to anger in the face of persistence. She had gained a reputation as rather unapproachable over the years and had actually welcomed the title of prude to help her keep her horrible secret. Less sensitive boys had at one time or another called her gay or les, and she even let that pass in favor of challenging anyone to look at her life.

Dillon had made reservations for nine-thirty at Archie Brennen's, a classy three-story restored historical landmark home that had been converted into one of Spokane's finest restaurants—with prices to match. The game had started at an uncharacteristically early time—six-thirty—so Jen had plenty of time to shower and wind down before they headed over. She was to change in Coach Sherman's office as soon as the other players were gone.

The gym was empty except for the janitor, sweeping up the portion of the floor that had been earlier covered by the collapsible bleachers; Coach Sherman, who sat at the empty scorer's table, working up the team stats; and Dillon, who waited patiently, if nervously, for Jen to get changed.

"You guys are going someplace nice, huh?" Coach said, appraising Dillon's leather sports coat and newly pressed jeans.

"Yeah, Brennen's."

"Ooh. Big spender."

Dillon raised his eyebrows but said nothing. He'd been on plenty of dates in his time, but this one made him jittery, even to talk about.

"Gonna have her in by team curfew?" Coach teased.

"Easy," Dillon said, glad to have Kathy keep things on a light note. "Wouldn't do to have the trainer undermining the team rules and regs."

"Rules and regs are off," Coach said more seriously. "Unless you make more money than I think you do, you're in for a major capital outlay. You guys just have a good time. It won't hurt Jennifer a bit to lighten up a little."

Dillon blew out a sigh. "Won't hurt Dillon a bit to lighten up a little right now either," he said. "This might be a big mistake. My gut is hopping around like a rabbit on an anthill."

Coach shrugged and smiled. "Could be love," she said. "Whatever that is."

At Brennen's Dillon ordered steamed clams for an appetizer and their best nonalcoholic champagne, pulling out every trick of etiquette his father and mother had drilled into his head from the day he was old enough to drop a spoonful of mashed peas three feet to the rug. He was smooth as polished leather, except he couldn't think of anything to say that didn't sound like elevator talk.

"Pretty good game," he said over the salad.

Jen smiled. "Pretty good. Not much to it really."

"Rather have a tougher game going into the tournament?"

Jen shrugged. "I don't know that it matters really. Once the tournament starts, I can't even remember the season."

Neither could take that conversation much farther, nor did they have better luck with the weather, the SATs or Jen's summer job prospects. Looking across the table at her, with the light so soft on her face and her hair falling easily on her shoulders and over her silky blouse, Dillon felt, clearly for the first time, the beginnings of a physical attraction, the part that had been missing, and his attempts at conversation became immediately more difficult. An hour and forty-five minutes from the time they were seated Dillon was better than fifty bucks in the hole and the "date" was a monumental bust.

When he pulled up in front of Jen's house, Dillon shut down the engine and turned toward her, his back against the door, elbow resting on the steering wheel. He said, "Maybe this wasn't as great an idea as it seemed when I had it."

Jen's head was down, staring at her hands in her lap. "It wasn't you. I think I don't play this part very well."

Dillon stared out the front window a second, tapping his fingers lightly on the steering wheel, thinking. "So what do you want to do?"

"What do you mean?"

"I don't know for sure. The day I met you I had this really strong feeling of connection, almost like I already knew you. It was like I used to have with Stacy when I was a kid. I guess I just naturally thought I was supposed to do something about it."

"Well, you have. We spend a lot of time together. I feel the connection, too, Dillon."

"So," Dillon said, looking back at her, "what's wrong with this picture? I see you. You see me. We're attracted to each other. You're pretty—beautiful, actually—and there are uglier guys in the world than I. We're both smart; we like the same things. I'm a boy; you're a girl. Everything works out like a storybook until we go on a date, where we treat each other like extraterrestrials." He shook his head. "I don't get it."

Jennifer looked at him, and her face softened. "There are things about me you don't know, Dillon. I'm not going to tell you what they are, not now anyway. But if you knew, they would help it make sense, I think."

He nodded slowly, looking into her eyes. He trusted what she said, and the *way* she said it let him know not to push.

"What I need for you to do is not to make some big complicated deal out of this, okay?

Dillon said okay without knowing exactly what he was saying. It *was* a complicated deal.

"I need you to be in my life," Jen said. "But I can't let us be in love. At least not like most people think of it. Not physically anyway. Not now. I can let you touch my heart, you've done that from the first day; but I can't let you touch my body, and I guess that's what 'dates' are all about."

Dillon put his hands flat on the ceiling. "So what do you want me to do?"

"Just what you've been doing, if you can. Care about me. Spend time with me. Fix my wounds on the court."

Dillon sat, bewildered. Finally, when Jen remained quiet, he said, "Hell, I can do that. I *been* doing that." He squinted as if that would help him see things more clearly. "Jen, would you tell me something?"

"If I can."

"Do I appeal to you? I mean, do you think I'm good-looking or funny or any of whatever it is that attracts girls to guys?"

She laughed. "Of course I do. I think you're all those things. I'm not blind and deaf. I'm just screwed up."

"That's all, huh, just screwed up."

"That's all."

"Will you make me a deal?"

"What?"

He took a deep breath. "Will you tell me about it someday?"

Jen looked down. "I don't know. Someday maybe."

Dillon hesitated, his head nodding like a toy dog in the back of a '55 Chevy. "I guess I thought we'd be more than friends."

Jen touched his hand, held it a second, and said, "There's no such thing as more than friends."

There is when you're as horny as I am, Dillon thought, but he only nodded.

"So, how did your date with Jen go?" Coach asked. Dillon stood in the back of her office, folding towels, while Coach sorted out uniforms.

"You remember high school, Coach?" he asked.

"Vaguely. But I asked you first. How did your date go?"

"I'm going to tell you," he said, "but I need to put it in context." He walked to her desk with a pile of towels and dropped them on the top. "When you were in high school, did things turn out like you expected them to?"

"Well, I expected to get a D in Latin, and I got it. What things do you mean?"

"*Any* damn thing," Dillon said in exasperation, continuing to fold. "The date was a bust. The second we were 'going out' neither of us could think of a thing to say. Imagine *me* not thinking of something to say. That's like A. J. Foyt being afraid to drive home from the track. I blew fifty bucks on a meal I can't even remember the taste of because I was concentrating so hard on how shitty things were going."

"You should start slower," Coach said. "Next time go to Burger King."

"No kidding. But we had a good talk afterward, and I thought things were fine. I mean, basically she said she wanted me to be her friend, and isn't looking for any others, really, but we just can't act like one of us is a girl and one is a guy."

Coach laughed. "Cuts down on your chances for contracting anything unpleasant, in a genital sense, I mean." She thought a second. "You don't have an agreement that you won't go out on dates, do you?"

"No," Dillon said. "But I don't really feel like it. For

one thing, I started getting these really strong feelings—you know, like sexual—somewhere there in the main course. That's never happened before with Jen. I can't tell if I'm screwed up because something's wrong with me or if I'm screwed up because of circumstances. The only other girl I'd consider going out with is in love with my dead brother." He shook his head. "I think there's a fairly good chance I'm going to end up in some obscure religious order."

"Might have to clean up a little of your impulsiveness," Coach said.

"And speaking of girls in love with my dead brother," Dillon went on, intent on exploring the rest of what seemed just a little bizarre in his life, "guess what else I think I found out."

"What else do you think you found out?" Coach asked, stacking the jerseys in one pile and starting in on the shorts.

"Have you seen Stacy Ryder's adopted brother?"

"Once," Coach said. "She brought him to school."

Dillon pulled out a wallet-sized snapshot. "Does this little booger look familiar?" he asked.

"It looks like Stacy's brother," she said.

"Yes, it does," he said. "Want to know who it really is?"

"You're telling me it's not Stacy's brother," Coach said. "So who is it really?"

"It's goddamn *me*," Dillon said. "And you know what? I've seen Stacy's cousin, and she doesn't look one little bit like me, and neither does anyone in her family."

"What're you saying?"

"I'm saying that ain't no adopted baby. I'm saying that's my brother's baby. Ryan Ryder is my freaking *nephew*."

Coach stopped sorting. "Dillon, you don't know that. You should be a little bit careful before you fly off with some wild idea. A lot of babies look alike."

"I'm not flying off," Dillon said. "I mean I'm not going to do anything about it. I *can't* do anything about it. But I can sure check it out with Stacy."

Coach shrugged.

"Do you think I should?" Dillon asked.

"Don't we have a *counselor* at this school?" Coach asked back. "Why are you asking me all this?"

"Yeah, we have a counselor. They sent me to her after Preston killed himself. I think she's better at helping kids choose a college."

Coach put her things aside and sat on her desk, motioning for Dillon to sit in her chair. "So, what do you want from me?" she asked.

"Advice," he said. "Tell me what to do."

"I don't do that. I *never* do that. You know a minute ago when you asked me if anything turned out the way I expected it to?"

"Yeah."

Coach Sherman watched Dillon for a moment, searched his eyes as if struggling with whether or not to go on with this, then: "Dillon, why do you think I'm not married?"

"I don't know. Never found anybody good enough, I guess."

Coach smiled. "Is that what you guess? It's a good thing you're cute, Dillon, because you're not going to make it with insight. I'm not married because I could never make a relationship work; never found anyone who had the same expectations that I have. All my life I was told by my parents and my teachers and my friends how women were supposed to be, but I could never pull it off because it wasn't how *I* was." She shook her head and laughed. "High school was a horror show for me. I spent the whole time thinking something was wrong with me because I wouldn't play the game the way it was laid out. One of the reasons I became a teacher was to see if I could change that for some kids."

"What about that TV guy? Wayne whatever. You guys get along pretty well, don't you?"

Coach nodded. "We get along fine. But you'll notice you don't see us together all that often. It's certainly not what you'd call a full-time relationship. I love it this way. And so does Wayne. But it's certainly not what's considered 'normal' and it's certainly not what I expected I would want at forty-two years old back when I was in high school."

Dillon felt the need to put Coach's information into a context he could understand. "So do you think you'll get together—you know, completely?"

"Dillon, what do you want from me?"

"Like I said, I thought I wanted advice."

"About what?"

"About Stacy. About Jen. Things just seem so out of control."

"It would just be bad advice," Coach said. "But maybe I can help a little."

"A little is better than nothing."

"Dillon, all you have in this world, really, are your responses to it. Responses to your feelings and responses to what comes in from outside. You know how adults are always trying to get you to 'take responsibility? That's all responsibility is, responding to the world, owning your responses. It isn't about taking blame or finding out if something's your fault."

"Okay," Dillon said. She always made him think.

"You have no control over the world. You have no control over anyone but you. You can't control how Stacy feels about you or whether she had your brother's baby. You can't control what's gone on in Jennifer's life or how she's reacting to that. There's nothing in the world outside yourself you can control. Winter's cold, summer's warm. Things fall from high places, they break. You lie, trust goes. Truth stays the same, Dillon. Truth is simply what is. It doesn't have to be believed to exist. Only our responses change."

"I know this helps me," Dillon said, "but I don't know how."

"You always want to fight, but you never want to fight at *home*, you always want to fight on foreign soil. The wars with Caldwell, the wars about your brother, about your mom leaving. The war to make things *fair* all the time, to make Stacy and Jennifer fit into something you're familiar with. All things you have no control over. That's not where the war is, Dillon." She pounded her chest lightly with her fist. "The war's in here."

Dillon looked down. Though he didn't completely

understand, something hit close to home because he was embarrassed, like back in the fourth grade when he found he'd been beating on a kid for fifteen minutes who *hadn't* stolen his bike.

"Your responses are all you have," Coach said again. "It's exactly the same thing I tell the girls in basketball, but it's easier to understand there because there are rules and an identified playing field. In basketball, when you respond well to what you see, you play a good game. You play a *great* game when you're able to respond to something you've never seen before, something brand-new."

The light switched on briefly. "You mean like falling in love in a way nobody ever told you about?"

Coach smiled. "I mean like falling in love in a way nobody ever told you about."

Dillon took a deep breath. "But I don't know how to respond well to that."

Coach shrugged. "So I guess you go by feel. The good part is, you go with whatever works. There's no precedent, so as long as you agree with whoever else is involved, you can't be wrong. That part I can tell you from experience."

Dillon's mind reeled. He'd been looking for simplicity. This *was* simple, though certainly not what he thought he'd asked for. Finally he said, "You're basically saying I'll do what I'm going to do, right?"

"Right. And that you need to own up to it, to yourself. You can be active or passive about your choices, and you can even trick yourself into thinking it's all out of your control, but every move you make is yours."

As usual, when Dillon spelunked in Coach Sherman's dimly lit spiritual cave he came away with artifacts he didn't immediately understand. He finished folding the towels and stuffed them into the footlocker in silence, though a very busy conversation rattled on in his head. He started to leave, then turned around at the door and walked over to Coach and hugged her.

"You're one tough chick," he said.

"Watch it," she said back as he ambled out the door.

CHAPTER 9

Dear Preston,

Well, brother, old Dillon decided to take the bull by the horns and get this all out on the table—aboveboard, as it were—just to see what the hell it looked like in the light of day as opposed to inside the bottomless caverns of my paranoic imagination. I billed it as a friendly get-together, a chance for my two best friends to meet and begin to get to know each other, secretly hoping that one area of conversation would lead to another, with my expert guidance, and I'd get some information out and some questions answered.

I've been absolutely haunted for the past few days, since figuring out that Ryan Ryder is really Ryan Hemingway and following a conversation I had with Coach about—for lack of a better description—how life works or doesn't work. I was really intrigued by her idea that if I keep my mind on myself and my own reactions to the world, I can have complete control, that trying to control everything outside me is what keeps me stuck and completely out of control. Opposites at work, I think, maybe Stacy's Chinese handcuffs. Who knows? I may be the world's next really great philosopher. Then again, I may be the world's next really great jerk. It's a crapshoot, I tell you. But it can't hurt, because there exists in this the possibility that I'll be able to put you in your rightful place.

Anyway, I was supposed to pick Jen up at her place· ("Just honk, don't come in." Hell, Dad would be tempted to slap the back of my head till my nose bled if he saw me do that. "You walk right up to the door, son, don't be disrespectful. Young ladies deserve respect." Remember that?) and take her to the library for an hour and a half, then meet Stacy and Ryan over at Jackie's Home Cookin' for some pie and ice cream.

When I picked Jen up, I saw her stepdad in the doorway. I can't remember if I thought he looked ominous standing there, but I'm blessed with retroactive memory (whatever I remember at this moment is the way I've always remembered it), and after hearing Jen's stories tonight, I'm sure he looked *extremely* ominous. And I'm going to get him. One way or another. I'll honor the promise I made to Jen and not blow it all sky-high, but I'm going to get him.

You can't treat people like that and be allowed to grow old peacefully and die. You have to eat shit first.

It's too bad you didn't stay around for the fireworks, Pres (though a lot of them might not have gone off in the first place if you had). This was one of the most incredible nights I've ever spent, and it all happened in my parked car and over pie and ice cream at Jackie's. Compared with this, the night the Warlocks came after me was a cakewalk.

We drove to the library, and Jen was real quiet. I thought she was lost in the upcoming district tournament, so I left her alone, and about the only conversation we had was to ask each other questions for the contemporary world problems test tomorrow. We cut the study time short and decided to go on over to the restaurant early because we really weren't getting anywhere studying. Between us we knew enough answers for a strong B+, so we'll probably sit close and cheat. Stacy might even be able to come up with enough extras for an A. It doesn't really matter, though.

Jen was real distracted on the ride over, and I asked her if she wanted to skip it and get together with Stacy some other time.

She said, "No, I don't want to go home yet. My sister's not there tonight."

That didn't make much sense to me, but I didn't pay any attention because she seemed so out of it, so far away.

I asked if there was anything I could help with.

She was staring out her side window and just shook her head.

God, Pres. It really makes me nuts when she gets like that, and I told her how I feel so helpless.

She didn't say anything, just kept staring out the window.

Finally I said, "God damn it, Jen, tell me *something*. This is driving me crazy, I'm serious. I can handle that we aren't lovers, and I can handle being your friend; but I can't be a good friend if I don't know what your *pain* is all about. You're in so much pain sometimes. . . ."

Without turning toward me, without moving a muscle, she said, "My stepdad messes with me." She said that, Pres.

"What?"

"You wanted to know what all my pain is. My stepdad messes with me."

"What do you mean, messes with you? You mean, *messes* with you?"

"I mean, he's been having sex with me," she said. "For a long time."

All the missing parts I'd been digging blindly for fell into place like tumblers in a fine combination lock, and the huge metal door of my consciousness swung open; but all I could say was "Je-sus Christ."

She said, "He hasn't had much to do with it."

"I'll bet. Why haven't you told somebody?"

Jen gave a little snort, and from the back I watched her head turn slowly from side to side. "Like who, Dillon?"

"Well, I mean, they have child protective services. You could tell the cops."

Jen still hadn't looked at me. "I did that. Back in Chicago."

"What happened?"

She let out this sigh, Pres, and I swear she sounded eighty years old, and she said, "Child Protective Services isn't for rich people, and it isn't for smart people. My stepdad was one of the top family law practitioners in Chicago, and he's one of the top family law practitioners here. He was way smarter than they were. They didn't have a chance. I was eleven years old, and he made them look like fools and me look like a stupid liar."

I stopped the car in front of Jackie's and turned off the engine, reached across the seat to touch her. Her body tightened like a steel cable, and she said, "Please . . ."

"Okay," I said. "What can I do?"

"You can listen and promise not to do anything. And promise not to feel sorry for me."

You have no idea how hard a promise that was to make,

but I knew Jen was in control here. Even so, I couldn't *imagine* not doing anything.

"Dillon," she said into my silence, "don't even *think* you can do something. He's untouchable. And he's mean beyond anything you can imagine."

"I'm not afraid of him, Jen."

She whirled, and I thought she was going to take my head right off my shoulders. "*I'm* afraid of him," she whispered. "He's a killer. I have a mother and a sister that he'd do away with in a heartbeat. Now I'm asking you to listen to me and promise you won't try to do anything. I need somebody to listen to me. You're the only one there is." And then she took the sides of my face in her hands and said, "If you try to do *anything* you'll cease to exist in my universe. I swear it."

"Okay," I said, "I can do that. I can listen." I knew it would be hard, but I thought I could do it.

Her shoulders slumped, and she let out a little air; relaxed a bit, I think. "I tried CPS in Chicago," she said again. "It took me two years to get up the guts. After the first time he . . . well, after the first time, he came into my room with a Polaroid picture of my dog's head under his boot, wedged next to the car tire, and told me if I ever told anyone, the dog would have an accident. The day I reported it he tied the dog to the back bumper and ran over her and left her on the porch. You couldn't even recognize her face. He ran right over her head." I can't tell you how I felt, Pres. I just wanted to go over to her place and kill him. I swear, if she'd said the word, I would have.

She started to tremble, and I reached for her again; but she pulled away.

"He'd already told me he'd do something to Mom and my sister, but I believed what the people at school said about how sex abusers sometimes make scary threats. I believed if I told, someone would do something."

"What happened?"

"To make a long, ugly story short, he had no trouble convincing my mom I was lying because she would have done anything to keep him, even though he beat her up all the time. I hate her, Dillon. And I hate that I love her. I can't stand to stay away because of what he does to her. I don't know why he doesn't hit her as much when I'm there, but he doesn't. If I didn't care about her, I'd take my sister and leave. But I can't. I don't know why, but I just can't. I think he'd kill her. I mean, really beat her to death. I saw him kick her so hard in the stomach one night I thought she was going to explode. You know what I remember most about living in Chicago?" Jen laughed and shook her head. "I remember standing in the snow with my sister and my mother in the woods. We lived on the outskirts. Dawn and I were the fastest packers in the world. We could have worked for Bekins. That bastard would get drunk and beat Mom almost unconscious, then storm out. Every time she promised we were leaving and never coming back. 'Get your things together, girls, we're getting out.'" Jen mimicked her mother with such astonishing contempt that my guts reeled, Pres. I've never seen such hate. And she *stays*.

It was scary. She kept talking like she was back there. "We'd be packed in fifteen minutes and out the door. We had to stay away from the roads because T.B. would always come back quick and look for us. I *know* he was terrified we'd blow his cover and he'd be ruined. Mom and Dawn and I would stay away from the roads and cut through the woods." Tears started to roll down Jen's cheeks. I wanted to do something to help. I'd have done *anything*. But there was nothing. She kept right on talking. "I remember Dawn up to her waist in snow, dragging her suitcase, just crying and dragging it. She was the toughest little shit you'd ever want to meet; but pretty soon she'd collapse, and I'd carry her suitcase, too."

I couldn't believe it. I said, "But your mom didn't tell?"

Jen just shook her head. "We'd always go to a motel or someplace where no one knew us. We never went to any of her friends or to a battered woman's shelter or anything like that. By morning Mom would already be getting us ready to go home, telling us things would be better, that the fight was her fault and if she'd quit nagging all the time, T.B. would stop. The time right before I told, I remember standing in the middle of the motel screaming at her. I was eleven years old, and I was screaming that my mother was a stupid bitch."

"What'd she do?"

"She slapped me and told me to be quiet."

"So what happened when you told?"

Jen looked down at her hands. Her fingers were knotted, and even in the darkness of your van I could see her knuckles were almost white. "They did an investigation. Took me out of the house and put me in foster care for a little while. I actually thought I'd done the right thing, that finally this nightmare would be over, but it was killing me that Dawn was still there. They didn't take Dawn. I don't know why unless they didn't believe me from the start. Anyway, both Mom and T.B. told CPS and the cops that I'd been sexually abused by my real dad, which was true, and that I'd always resented T.B. and the only reason they could think that I'd say such a thing about him was that I knew it would get him in trouble and that I was using it to get him out."

"Jesus, it *worked*?"

"Dillon, this guy is *good*. He never loses. He represents some of the real slime of the universe in divorce cases, and he *never* loses. You see the house we live in? We're *rich*. And we're rich because he's good. I was back home in less than a week. I could see it coming. When she picked me up, the caseworker was right there telling me she'd take care of me and make sure I was protected and I could call her anytime, and within two days she was grilling me like a convict. I just gave up. I said, 'Send me back. You're going to do it anyway. Just hurry up.'"

"What about Dawn? Why didn't she tell?" I asked.

"Mom and T.B. got to her. There was a lot she didn't see. She didn't know anything about the sexual stuff. She might have even thought I was making that up to get rid of him. I was real mad at her for a while, but she was young. And really confused."

"So that was it? I mean, they just decided you were lying?"

"That was it. He handled those people like school kids. They never even saw his temper. He was 'just as concerned' as they were and just as worried about my traumatic past with my real dad, and he could even see why I'd say what I said; but boy, it really gave him a scare there for a while, 'cause he knew what society thinks about sex abuse. He even went down to their office one day to get the name of some good therapists he might be able to send me to to help me work things out. Money was no object. He cared only about my well-being . . . shit." She took a deep breath and nodded toward the entrance of the restaurant. "Let's go in."

I sat against the car door, soaked in sweat from hearing her story. I thought *I* had the worst story in the world to tell, but this just bowled me over. "Wait for just a minute," I said. I just *couldn't* let it ride. "We have to do something."

She flared again. "*No*, Dillon. You promised. You're either going to be a person I trust or not. If not, get out of here."

I raised my hands. "Okay, okay," I said, but I could barely get my teeth ungritted. "I promised. You can trust me. But I don't know what to do. I can't stand leaving you there. I can't stand the thought that he's "

Jen laughed and said, "Don't worry. I'm *not* there. My body's there, but I perfected the art of mental evacuation long, long ago. Clear back with my dad . . ."

Stacy's car pulled into the parking lot by the side of the restaurant then, and she stepped out, waved, and opened the back door to remove Ryan from the car seat. I said, "Listen, if you don't want to go in, I can take you home and come back."

She said, "No, I'm okay. All this news isn't blowing *me* away. I've known it for years. I'd like to get to know Stacy."

Boy, I haven't been that agitated for a *long* time, maybe

since you died. All the ideas I had about this get-together turning into an informational clearinghouse were intensified by about seven thousand. I couldn't tell Stacy what I'd learned from Jen; but Stace is a reader of ambience, and she knew the mood before we'd all sat down. She also seemed to have some of that same kind of immediate connection with Jen that I'd had, so by the time the pie was on the table we were about three days into some serious talk, except for Ryan, of course, who was deeply into his pie art.

I felt this incredible need to *purge*, and the natural place to start was with my complicity in your death. It was the only thing powerful enough to get the conversation where I wanted it, and I thought it might establish trust. Once again, little big brother, I used you. I told them how I knew something was wrong but I let it go. And that once I got over the shock, a part of me was almost *glad* you did it. I've never said that before to anyone. I've thought it, and I've written it to you; but I've never actually heard those words. They threw me, but it was still true. I wouldn't have wanted your life for anything in the world, and if I'd had it, I'm not a bit sure I wouldn't have taken the same road.

Then I looked at Stacy and reached into my backpack. I pulled out the picture of me in the restaurant when I was a year old and handed it to her. I said, "The beat goes on."

Stacy just smiled and sort of nodded. "That Preston?"

"Actually," I said, "it's me."

"No difference, really. The only reason I haven't told everyone is my parents," she said. "I'm surprised anyone bought that story for fifteen seconds. I'm embarrassed to have to tell it."

Jen looked confused.

Stacy touched her knee and told it all. "Dillon's brother was Ryan's dad." She pushed her pie around the plate absently with her fork for a second, and Ryan took that as an indication that she wanted him to put a full handprint into it, which he did. The temperature of the ice cream surprised him a bit, but his shocked look turned quickly to glee as he stuck his hand into his mouth. Little bugger didn't have an idea what was being said would probably change his life forever. He just wanted more of that pie. And Stace went right on. "The crazy part is I did it on purpose. I lied and left my diaphragm home. Preston was so far gone and so far away from *me* that I was sure I was losing him forever. I don't even know what I was in love with, probably just memories, because there sure wasn't anything left coming from him." She nodded toward Ryan. "Sometimes I think I had him to give myself a little Preston." She closed her eyes. "That's sick." That's what she said, Pres. I know it won't exactly make you the happiest corpse in the world, but we're telling all here.

I sat in the booth and looked at Ryan, who leaned against Stacy, reaching for more of her pie, still untouched by all of this, and I said, "For a little shit, Preston made a lot of noise on the way out, huh?"

Stacy's eyes remained closed. "You know, Dillon, you said part of it might be your fault, knowing how crazy he looked that day and all."

"Yeah."

"Well, you get only half the blame because he killed himself the day after I told him I was pregnant." Tears started down her face, and Ryan tried to put his finger to one of them, leaving a perfect strawberry-rhubarb and ice cream fingerprint. "You might have provided the murder weapon, but I supplied the motive." She opened her eyes again and looked at Ryan. "I love this little snotmaker," she said, "but it might have been a mistake. I don't know what he needs half the time, and sometimes when I look at him and start thinking about Preston, I want to strangle him. But another part of me says I'd do it all again."

So you see, Pres, you left things in a mess. I wish to hell I could make you come back and own your part of it all; but you made the great escape, and there's no turning that back. It's four o'clock in the morning now, and you're probably glad you're dead, so you really don't have to read this. My ghost of a nephew is home licking the rest of Stacy's pie off his fingers, dreaming of new ways to foul his Jockey shorts; Jennifer, who I just love so much after tonight, I can barely stand it, is in her bed thanking God her house was dark when she got home and more than likely her asshole of a stepdad was asleep. Stacy and I both think we killed you, and I'm sitting here wondering what appropriate *responses* to all this would be, and I can't ask the one person in the world—Coach—who might be able to help me with that because before the night was over, I'd promised everyone I wouldn't tell *anything* I heard tonight.

When I let Jen off, she was warmer to me, actually brushed the side of my face with hers, and told me she was sorry she had to be so cold. It came to me that the reason I've never felt much for her physically before is she hasn't offered *any* kind of target for that.

So at least I'm not crazy there.

The place I may be *really* crazy is that from the instant I knew her stepdad was messing with her, I felt this tremendous desire for her. I can't ever tell anyone alive that, and I don't have a clue what to do with it. Responses are one thing; impulses are another. I'm gonna have to watch myself like a hawk.

Hell, I'm going to bed.

Dillon

CHAPTER 10

Dillon fell onto his bed, exhausted. Earlier in the evening he had spent several hours with Jennifer and Stacy and Stacy's son, Ryan, clearing the decks, and had come home so conflicted and confused that he couldn't concentrate on TV or hold a conversation with his dad or read without vivid images of Jennifer and her stepdad or of Preston blowing his head off. Finally he pulled on his winter running gear—long johns under sweatpants, two sweatshirts (one crew-necked and one hooded) over a long-sleeved running shirt, and gloves—and hit the dark, snowy streets in an attempt to run some of it off. Approximately an inch of newly fallen snow covered the streets, and the dark skies still spit flurries as he ran, so his relatively new Nike Airs gripped the road well, giving him a feeling of power as he ran. Available light glowed dimly off the new snow, and he had no trouble seeing his trail in the night, even on the four-mile loop through Three Forks Regional Park, where a high ridge blocked the lights of the city. He found his pace quickly, permitting his mind to run to the gentle rhythm of his waffle treads pushing into the snowy cushion.

A little more than an hour—and ten miles—after his onset, Dillon silently stripped off his sweat-soaked gear inside the enclosed porch and slipped through the house to the bathtub, not one of his dilemmas resolved, but at least physically more at peace. His father had long since stopped worrying about him when he disappeared on his late-night training excursions, and nothing stirred in the quiet house. For several hours he wrote in his journal before reaching this expended state in which he felt he could merely drop onto the bed and become unconscious. But still, he could not sleep, feeling he had set in motion forces he not only couldn't *control* but possibly couldn't contend with. He remembered the number of times he'd seen the cheap mahogany plaque on the desk in his dad's study: THE UNEXAMINED LIFE IS NOT WORTH LIVING.

So when it's examined, he thought, *what then?* He knew how to examine, but he didn't know how to evaluate. He would ask his dad, soon, what the plaque meant to him, a man whose family had all but deserted him, who must feel the pain of loss so tremendously that he could only close it off. A burst of guilt filled Dillon, triggered somehow by the flash of Ryan Ryder across the screen behind his eyes. Ryan Ryder, the next generation. You couldn't very well consider the next without considering the last. Dillon was suddenly aware he had left his father to figure it all out for himself. He was such a quiet man, seemingly so *strong* that Dillon never once thought to ask after *his* pain. What must it be like to watch everything you'd worked for for the past twenty-two years crumble before your eyes? Since Dillon could remember, his father had been a jack-of-many-trades, primarily a mail and freight man, contracting with the post office to haul into tiny mountain towns on the edges of the Idaho Primitive Area out of Three Forks, which stood only a few miles from the Washington-Idaho border. But Dillon could also remember his father at different times cleaning furnaces and building cabinets and taking in accounting work for small businesses, and he was aware that he'd never known if the Hemingways were rich people or poor people. He didn't know how his father went about taking care of the family. There was always enough, and no more than that was said. He remembered his father teaching a class out at Three Forks Community College, though he had no idea what subject material was involved. Dillon suddenly felt tremendously neglectful that he had never queried his father at least enough to let his dad know he was important to him. He would do that, he thought, soon. A boy's examined life needed to include his father.

As he contemplated his irresponsibility over the past two years, and as his muscles began to relax out of pure physical and emotional exhaustion, his mind began to drift and settled on the one time when his irresponsibility nearly resulted in *real* trouble, on the night the Warlocks came after him.

<<<>>>

Dillon is driving from Chief Joseph toward home by one of several alternative routes he's established in the past few days. It's three days after the last of the nocturnal acts of vandalism on Chief Joe, and he's acutely aware that the bikers haven't forgotten his feeble attempt at voodoo or, more important, his injection of a foreign substance into their meticulously kept engines. He is also aware that these guys have been linked, though not conclusively, to at least two killings and several disappearances over the past five years. They are dangerous men, not to be fooled with.

He has also, with the passage of a little time—very

little time, in fact—lost contact with some of the rage and zeal required to allow him to perform the act in the first place, and he is, quite frankly, scared to death that they'll catch him off guard somewhere and make quick work of him. After his second day of secret worry he told his dad, expecting to have his butt chewed to shreds, but Caulder was so broken by his own losses and so filled with the same rage coursing through Dillon's veins that he merely listened intently to the story, nodded, and cautioned Dillon to be very careful. Late that night Dillon came partway down the stairs after hearing unusual noises, only to find his father examining and loading a shotgun and a 30.06 rifle.

But the Warlocks didn't come.

So now Dillon looks into his rearview mirror almost as often as he looks out the windshield, expecting at any moment to see it filled with Harleys, storming in to surround him.

It's early evening, still light, with moderately heavy traffic still flowing on Ash Street, his main route home for tonight. It happens roughly the way he expected it to, first one bike in the mirror, mounted by a behemoth of a man behind mirrored sunglasses, his long dark hair whipping in the wind. The giant removes something from his belt and speaks into it, and within minutes he is joined by others.

Dillon's heart blasts off, and he's instantly scanning for an escape route; but the traffic clogs all possibilities, and he possesses none of the driving skills of a Hollywood stunt actor or the cockpit arrogance it would take even to consider that he could perform the lightning maneuvers required to lose a motorcyclist in a four-year-old Dodge van. It's time to pay.

Several bikers merge from the side street ahead to cut him off, and in his rearview mirror he watches two bikes, one on each side, pull beside him, waving him over to the curb.

Through the driver's window one biker shouts, "Pull over, shithead. We want to talk."

He looks straight ahead, thinking what they want to talk about is where to dump the body. The biker lifts his leg high and stomps the frame of the van just below the door. He glances over involuntarily. The biker points to a side alley and yells, "Pull over!"

Dillon nods, signals, and turns across traffic into the alleyway. With no conscious idea of his intention and in sheer panic, he hits the gas as the rear tires touch the dirt, and gravel cascades back out onto the street. He shoots into the intersection at the next block at full speed, eyes closed, half expecting to be creamed by oncoming traffic; but miraculously he flies across the street into the next alley untouched, thinking he may have a chance if he can drive crazy enough long enough to be seen and reported to the police, or, better, if he happens on to a cop.

That thought is barely warm when two Harleys pull across the alley entrance on the next block and sit strad-dled, arms crossed. Dillon slams the van into reverse for a flying backward exit, but the story in the rearview mirror is the same; and he knows the motorized portion of this chase is winding down quickly.

In a flash he's out of the van and over the garbage Dumpster on the driver's side, streaking toward the street between two old buildings, thinking this is how he should have done it in the first place. He has a much better chance on foot. He veers right at the sidewalk, headed back the way he came, hoping to throw them off long enough to give himself running room, knowing if he can get three blocks, four at most, he'll be at the river, which is lined with trees and underbrush. They'll have a rough time finding him there. If worse comes to worst, he can hit the water. The river is cold and rough in places; but he'd rather take his chances with a few rapids and hard rocks than let these leviathan mothers get to him.

The Warlocks figure him out quickly and double

back, staying with him on the street with their bikes as he sprints down the sidewalk. Dillon tries to picture the river, the hiding places there, and where he can get in if he has to. A fifteen-foot chain-link fence topped with circular barbed wire runs between the path and the river, and he can't think where it ends, but if he can get to that path, the fence has to stop somewhere.

At the river he takes another right and sprints south on the path. The brush isn't as thick as he pictured it, but the path is narrow and rough, and none of the bikers comes down, three of them choosing rather to ride parallel to him on Park Drive. Dillon knows there are more; but all he can do now is hope to get to the water before they figure out where he's going.

Ahead the path widens, and he sees the end of the fence. The bikes roar just to his right on the street, but he's sure he can get into the water before they get to him. Suddenly the wide spot in the path is filled with Warlocks. Most are on foot, and they're coming toward him. He skids to a stop and reverses direction, only to encounter an equal number moving through the brush to the path. They're all smiling—had him all the way. Up through the bushes the street is filled with bikes, and behind him is the fence. Trapped. He whirls and bolts for the fence, scaling frantically toward the barbed wire, which he finds to be thick and rigid. There's no way through it without shredding himself. He hangs from the top of the fence until his arms give out, then drops to the ground in a heap.

A voice above him, deep and mean, says, "We just want to talk to you, shithead."

The night before the chase, in the bowels of the Dragon tavern, the Warlocks held an informal meeting. It began with a conversation between Wolf and an angular, sinewy biker named Fat Jack. Jack, nearly forty, with long, stringy hair hanging in oily strands from an almost perfect bald beanie in his crown, reached into his breast pocket, pulled out a Baggie of coke, and strung out a few lines onto the table. "We done with the petty bullshit on the high school?" he asked, laying one end of his straw near his nose and approaching the coke line with the other.

"Yeah," Wolf said. "Enough's enough. No sense wasting any more time."

"What about Hemingway's brother?"

Wolf shrugged. "Boy's got to pay. We can't let no punks get away with butcherin' our hogs."

"Messed up mine pretty good," Fat Jack said. "I wanna piece of that kid."

Wolf smiled and nodded. "You'll get it. We'll all get it. No hurry, we can take our time. He's gotta be sweatin' rabbit pellets about now, wonderin' when we're comin'."

Jack lined up the coke, and both men snorted quickly, their straws resembling rival vacuum cleaners in a TV commercial. They looked up simultaneously to see Marva, leaning knuckles first onto the table. Marva was a bit unusual in that she was the only female Warlock, and her admittance into the gang had caused hard feelings among some members. Several had actually dropped out to form a club of their own. How tough could a gang be if a *woman* could be full-fledged? But Marva was strong as a bull and tough as boiled owl and sported nearly as many tattoos as Wolf. None of that would have been enough to allow her member status had she not, on a cold late night three years ago, pulled Wolf out from under his flaming bike and actually reached inside a gash to stop the blood flow from a major artery in his leg. When the attending physician let Wolf know he certainly would have lost his leg—not to mention his life—were it not for Marva's quick thinking, Wolf told her he owed her one.

Within that second Marva said, "Okay. I want to ride with your chickenshit motorcycle gang." It wasn't what Wolf had expected; but he stayed with his word, and among the Warlocks, Wolf's word was law.

Marva reached for the straw and snorted a quick line of her own.

"Just talkin' about makin' some short work of the Hemingway kid," Wolf said.

Marva smiled, slowly looking from one to another of the two bikers. She shook her head. "You pusses don't know a class act when you see one. If it was up to me, I'd be askin' the little shithead if he wants to join up. Throw in bike lessons for free."

Fat Jack snorted. He was used to Marva's jerking everyone around. The only thing faster than her nose for the snow was her mouth. "Yeah," he said. "It's a real class act, messin' up five hogs. Kid was stupid. Nothin' more than terminal stupid."

"You say so, Jack," Marva said. She laughed again. "How many heroes you think it will take to teach this rough, tough high school boy a lesson?"

The question obviously didn't merit an answer. Both bikers only glared at her as Jack set up another set of tracks on the table. "What's the matter with you, bitch?" Wolf asked. "That punk messed up some good Harleys, then come in here pourin' his goddamn brother all over everything. You think we let shit like that go?"

"Like I said, you guys don't know a class act when you see it. We're *Warlocks,* right? Boy witches? What's that sweet little genius do but come in here and *haunt* our asses. You see the rest of these pusses after he left? Even you, Jack, brushin' shit off and movin' away from all the hauntin' like the bogeyman himself was in that Baggie."

Wolf thought a second and smiled. "Yeah, that was cool. He shouldn't have messed with the bikes, though."

"Maybe," Marva said, "but in his mind we killed his brother. And to tell the truth, he's not that far off. You remember what you did when Song Man said your old man was a queer, Wolf? Like to tore his head right off his skinny shoulders."

"Let it ride, Marva," Wolf said.

"You know," she said, "I don't mind that you guys are assholes. That's why I ride with you. What I don't like is that you're *stupid* assholes."

No other Warlock would even consider speaking to Wolf in that manner, and Marva did it with astonishing regularity.

"You got a million-dollar drug business going, plus a hundred other illegal activities cookin', and you're willing to risk it all to get even with a punk high school kid." She shook her head in disgust. "What do you think the newspapers are gonna do with it when this kid turns up beaten bloody or dead? Cops'll be on us like grease on Fat Jack's hair."

Wolf hadn't taken his eyes from her. "Forget it. The kid is meat."

"And the Warlocks are pusses," Marva said. That was pushing it, even for Marva, and she stood to walk to another table.

Somewhere in the night, through the cocaine-leaden, beer-soaked, angel-dusted haze, Marva's words worked their way to a soft spot in Wolf's brain and started a nest there. He began to let it be known through the evening that the Warlocks were off the Hemingway kid's case. It was challenged often enough, and Wolf made enough counterthreats, that the idea lodged in, and he would not let it go even in the semisober hours of early morning. Somehow, through Marva's words, a fraction of Dillon Hemingway's actions became heroic, and it was a big enough fraction to save his skin. But a line had to be drawn. Hemingway needed to know it was a line he would not be allowed to cross again.

Dillon lies on the ground, waiting for the worst. He can almost feel the first steel-toed boot boring deep into his gut, but instead is helped to his feet. His first instinct is to swing and try again to run; but he's gasping for air and flat beat, and something tells him to take his medicine and maybe he'll come out alive. He opens his eyes to see Wolf staring back, smiling. "Good run. Had you all the way, though."

Dillon raises his eyebrows, still trying to catch his wind. "I s'pose so," he says. "Thought I could make it to the river."

"You were gonna jump in the river?"

Dillon nods. "It was my only chance."

"Didn't you hear Eddie tell you we just wanted to talk?"

"Yeah," Dillon says. "I heard him."

"So why the hell didn't you stop?"

"I didn't believe him."

Wolf nods, still smiling. Finally he says, "Look, kid, I'm sorry your brother snuffed himself, okay? This is a shitload more energy than we wanted to spend to tell you everything's even. Long as you're done playing Lone Ranger." Wolf sticks a finger hard into Dillon's chest. "But don't mess with us again. You'll lose more than just wind."

Dillon puts his hands up in the air. "No more Lone Ranger," he says, so relieved he thinks his legs will give away. "I'm done."

Wolf nods again, looking Dillon straight in the eye. "You better be," he says. "You better be."

When the last biker disappears into the brush, headed for the street, Dillon sinks to his knees at the fence and throws up his lunch.

«<»»

Jennifer experienced the same order of insomnia as did Dillon after the conversation in the car, though she responded differently. Because her interior world had been so deeply invaded all her life, her consistent tendency took her *outside* for comfort, focusing on challenges, past and present. Introspection left her feeling empty and powerless, her sense of guilt for her sexual complicity with T.B. being so great. As many times as she told herself how much she hated it, and *him*, and as much as the weight of responsibility for her mother's and Dawn's very lives held her down, she could never get past her awareness of the soiled, obscene harpoon that lay wedged in her soul. Introspection lead to one question: What's wrong with me? How dirty and awful must I be to have *always* been someone's target? So she looked outside; she played games—basketball games.

She visualized the tough ones, saw her opponents at their best and herself at hers. She ran defensive sequences over and over until she could actually see herself moving to the right spot at exactly the right time. And she imagined games in the future, previews of the toughest coming attractions. She would visualize all possible situations. When the game rolled around, Jen owned her opponents. That was where she went on nights like tonight, when her life troubled her, the same place she went on the nights when T.B. came into her room.

But tonight she lay more than merely troubled; she was unable to get away. Tonight was the first time she had said anything about the continuing horror of her existence since she was eleven, when she had sounded the alarm only to have it silenced. And even though she trusted Dillon Hemingway more than anyone—with the possible exception of Coach—since she had trusted her grandfather, still, any leak in that stainless steel box around her heart sent waves of panic through her. Only in containment was there any real control. If her real feelings ever started spilling out, well, she might just discover the pit of her pain and rage to be bottomless.

It amazed her sometimes that she maintained as well as she did. She had read enough books and watched enough "Oprah" and "Donahue" to know she was probably badly emotionally damaged, but she often wondered how she'd ever been able to function at all. Generally credit for that went to her grandfather. Through all the hazy, indeed often blacked-out memories of her past, her grandfather stood strong and tall and clear. She had known what was healthy then, what was real.

And there was Sarah, the therapist she had been sent to just before she turned six, after her real father was sent away. Sarah was a big, earthy woman, and the person most responsible for helping her six-year-old mind understand that what had happened with her father was not her fault, that because his late-night visits sometimes felt a little bit good, she was not bad. Sarah had actually joined Jennifer in her pain and rage and jumped over the cliff with her.

«««»»»

"What do you want to be today, J. Maddy?" Sarah asks, and Jennifer looks around the room at the possibilities. Sarah has called her J. Maddy from the first day, over her mother's protests, and that has helped J. Maddy feel strong. Sarah believes it is important for children to feel strong.

"I want to be a baby," J. Maddy says now in answer to Sarah's question.

"Whose baby do you want to be?"

"Yours."

Sarah cradles J. Maddy in her arms like a forty-pound Baby Huey, handing her a bottle filled with juice, which J. Maddy puts in her mouth while she sinks into the powerful woman's chest. Sarah rocks and hums and sings nonsensical songs for a few minutes, and J. Maddy immerses herself further into her. Then J. Maddy pulls away and says, "I don't want to be a baby anymore." Sometimes it feels *so* good just to be held again for a little while. It was hard at first because Mommy wouldn't put up with it for a second and J. Maddy thought it was wrong—after all, she was six—but in Sarah's room it's safe, and nobody teases her or calls her names, and then after a while she feels strong and wants to go on to other things.

"Let's do noses," J. Maddy says suddenly, crawling off Sarah's lap as the bottle drops to the floor.

"Who wants to do noses with J. Maddy?" Sarah asks, and all of the other five children raise their hands.

"So get 'em," she says, and the bathroom boy runs to the cupboard and pulls out a large blue plastic box filled with rubber noses with elastic bands to fit around your head so they'll stay on, noses for every animal in the world and some that don't really exist, J. Maddy knows, like the dinosaur noses.

J. Maddy doesn't call the bathroom boy that; she just thinks it. His name is Jeremy, and lots of times when he goes into the bathroom, he talks about how bad dads pee-pee on him and then throw him in the garbage. Sometimes he throws a fit when he talks about it, and then he's not talking at all but screaming. The kids have played the "Bad Dad in the Bathroom" game over and over for Jeremy, and the bad dad gets handcuffed and thrown in jail behind paper bars in the playhouse, and sometimes he stays there and sometimes he kicks the bars away and comes after them. Jeremy usually plays the bad dad because it's his game, but sometimes he wants J. Maddy to be it. It's a hard game because sometimes it seems that nothing anybody does will keep the bad dad down.

J. Maddy called Jeremy the bathroom boy once, and he punched her in the eye. "You can tell Jeremy you don't like to be hit," Sarah said, at which time J. Maddy screamed those very words at him. "And you can tell J. Maddy you don't like to be called bathroom boy," Sarah said to Jeremy, and Jeremy screamed it right back at her.

It was understood.

Today J. Maddy chooses alligator noses for everyone, and even though Michael wants the elephant nose,

Sarah offers him the choice of wearing the elephant nose around his neck and the alligator nose over his face. That way, if there is emergent need of an elephant, Michael will be Johnny-on-the-spot.

Sarah makes an alligator nest of paper sticks and other indigenous swamp material, and the kids begin to crawl around on their bellies, making huge alligator sounds that really sound more like lions and tigers. J. Maddy is the mother alligator, Jeremy is the daddy alligator, and the other kids are kid alligators. Jeremy can't be in the nest because he hurts the kid alligators, but J. Maddy keeps going away to play or watch alligator television, and Daddy Alligator sneaks in and hurts the kids. Everyone knows J. Maddy's alligator game because they've played it at least as many times as the bathroom game. The kid alligators scream and Mommy Alligator comes back and Daddy Alligator slinks off, but then Mommy Alligator goes off and Daddy Alligator thinks of a new way to sneak up on the alligator kids. Finally Gail, who is playing the J. Maddy alligator, bops Jeremy with a bad daddy beaner—a large foam rubber club—and all the other alligators roar and get foam rubber clubs of their own, and J. Maddy switches with Gail so she can be J. Maddy alligator and Gail turns into the mad mom alligator and everyone beats Bad Dad Jeremy into the "Everblades." Then, to everyone's glee, J. Maddy unveils Grampa Alligator. She has a beard from an abandoned Uncle Sam costume to go with her alligator nose, and when Mommy Alligator and all the kid alligators just can't cut the mustard, Grampa Alligator takes over. It is understood that when Grampa Alligator shows himself, bad dads shake in their scaly boots. Only when she feels particularly powerful does she allow herself to call on Grampa Alligator.

And that's the way it is in J. Maddy's life for months. All the kids in the group have had bad dads; some have had *lots* of them, and the children have games for each. Some also have bad moms, and there are games for them, too. Sometimes the moms win, and sometimes the dads win. But sometimes the *kids* win. It's very hard work, but J. Maddy is starting to feel strong.

After extensive work with J. Maddy's mother, Sarah even sets up a time for J. Maddy to tell her mother how mad she is that her mother didn't protect her. Her mother is able to tell her she is sorry, that it was *her* fault and not J. Maddy's.

It is *such* a relief.

Over the next few months J. Maddy is able to tell

her mother things she thought she would have to hold inside her forever. There are tears and pain and nothing is easy, and sometimes J. Maddy dreads going in because she has something she knows will make her mother feel really bad, but each time they stay with it until it's all out in the open.

And with Sarah and the other kids, J. Maddy flies. Sometimes they're strong and sometimes they're weak; but they're always real and there are *no lies,* and Sarah just seems to join with them in every horror any kid wants to approach. J. Maddy loves Sarah, and she loves the other kids, and something in her heart is happy.

And then it's gone.

J. Maddy and her mother go into a big room in a big building one day, and there are people in suits and they use a lot of big words that J. Maddy doesn't understand; but it sounds like they're telling her mother that she's better now but that she should continue letting J. Maddy see Sarah, though she doesn't have to.

Linda promises that she will.

But when she doesn't have to, she doesn't. J. Maddy doesn't even really get to say goodbye to Sarah, her mother just keeps coming up with excuses not to take her, and pretty soon Sarah and the other children begin to fade into the dark caverns of her memory. Mom keeps promising to take her back, and she even hears her promise Sarah that on the phone one day; but they don't go, and J. Maddy starts feeling tricked again. Good things always go away. She fights with her mother about it and one day even gets slapped for calling her a big fat liar. Her mother immediately bursts into tears when she hits J. Maddy, and J. Maddy takes care of her, telling her it's okay and she won't tell anyone.

«««»»»

She jumped off with us, Jennifer thought, lying in the darkness. She remembered hating Sarah for a while because she thought Sarah was big and strong and powerful enough to come get her, to *make* her mother keep taking her back until she was finished. But no one could get through Linda Lawless's inertia. She just faded away and couldn't be touched. Sarah was powerful with Linda because Linda was isolated during that time; there were no men around. But men began to show up shortly after the day the people told Linda she was better, men J. Maddy didn't know, and though none of them really hurt her, many were strange and scary, and her mother left her alone in the house a lot to go with them.

The time is coming, Jennifer thought, to remember

what Sarah said to both me and my mother: that kids have an inalienable right to unconditional care, and parents who don't give it are breaking a spiritual law. She remembered those words as if Sarah had spoken them yesterday. Someday soon, Jen would have to abandon her mom for whatever fate lay in store. She'd take Dawn, too, because no kids could live in the poisonous environment T.B. and her mother provided, no matter how much money there was. But someday soon she'd have to do what Sarah had told her a long, long time ago, seemingly in another world: Let her mother be responsible for herself.

CHAPTER 11

Dillon walked into the kitchen, where his dad sat reading the paper over breakfast. Caulder Hemingway looked up and smiled, sliding the sports section to Dillon's usual spot at the table, and nodded toward the sink counter, where an open package of granola and a carton of milk stood waiting. "Didn't get to the dishes," his father said. "Have to rinse out a bowl for yourself."

"Need to get us a domestic," Dillon said back, shoving a plastic bowl under running water in a semivaliant attempt to wash out the SuperBond-like remains of *yesterday's* granola. He chiseled small bits loose with the handle of a spoon, semiseriously rinsed the bowl again, and filled it to the edges. "Surface tension," he said, carrying it carefully to the table so as not to break the scientific seal restraining the milk from overflow.

"We learned about it in fourth grade. Who says your educational tax dollars are going to waste?"

Caulder Hemingway smiled and shook his head slowly, returning to the front page.

Dillon ate a couple of bites of the granola, then laid his spoon carefully down beside the bowl. "Dad," he said.

"Hmmm?"

"How come we never talk about Preston?"

Caulder stared at him over the top of the paper, taken somewhat by surprise but considering the question.

"Or Mom. And Christy."

"I don't know why you don't talk about them," Caulder said, folding the newspaper in front of him. "I don't talk about them because I don't know what to say."

Dillon nodded slowly. "Yeah. Me, too."

"Do you want to talk about them?"

Dillon nodded again. "Yeah, I think I do."

His dad leaned forward, resting on his elbows. "Where do you want to start?"

"I'm not sure. It just seems like three years ago we were a family of five and then three and now two, and nobody ever said anything about how it happened. Or how anybody feels about it. Mom's same as you. When

I go over there, she acts like she's always lived there. Christy and I are the only ones who ever talk about it."

"What do you say?"

"Well, she just wonders what happened, and I make up things to tell her."

Caulder smiled. "To tell you the truth, son, I'm a little like Christy. Most of the time I wonder what happened, too."

Dillon merely watched his dad, wishing he were as clear about where he wanted the conversation to go as he had been last night lying in bed thinking about it.

"Much as I hate to say it," Caulder went on, "this family thing kind of took me by surprise. I mean from the beginning. I always thought if I put food on the table, kept a roof over our heads, didn't lose my temper too often, and set up a few family vacations, that I had the father part of this show pretty well covered."

"You did a lot more than that, Dad," Dillon said. "Look at all the things we learned from you." Dillon flashed back to nights in the distant past—back before grade school—lying out in the backyard under the stars, listening to his dad talk about time and space in a way he barely understood but utterly treasured, how the light that reached our eyes was really from long ago and that we could actually see back into the past by merely gazing upward on a starry night. When Dillon had pressed him, Caulder would say, "Just remember things aren't always as they appear," and let it go at that.

"Look at the things *you* learned from me," Caulder said. "I didn't do as well by your brother. Or Christy." Dillon's father closed his eyes and shook his head slowly. "He was the first, and I thought I had to do everything right, you know, make no mistakes with discipline and all that, and me just out of the service. Preston might just as well have been born into basic training." He smiled a tired smile. "I left the humor out. If I had it to do over again, I'd do a lot of things different."

"Like what?"

"Like paying attention. Like going with my instincts, tending to your mother." He laughed a short laugh. "She used to say I didn't care. She'd get all quiet, and I'd never ask what was wrong. She thought it was because I was 'insensitive,' as she put it, but really it was because I was scared there *was* something wrong. God knows I wouldn't have known how to fix it."

"It must be tough at first," Dillon said, "I mean, starting a family and everything."

Caulder laughed. "You wouldn't believe it, my boy. I swear to God I must have thought people were like Disney animals. I used to watch those wilderness pictures about bears and lions and prairie dogs and the like, and those animals just had their babies and fed 'em for a while and whopped 'em alongside the head when they screwed up, and the babies grew up just fine— except for the ones that got eaten. I thought it was just natural to know how to be a dad and a mate." He looked around the empty kitchen. "I was wrong. The thing, apart from opposing thumbs, that separates us from the rest of the animal kingdom is common sense. They got it; we don't."

Dillon was moved that his father would talk with him like this. It was an experience he'd not had before— one he'd longed for, more than he had known.

"You know, Dad," he said after a few seconds of considering the possibilities of sending Stacy to the zoo for parenting classes, "we can still be a family, you and me. It's not too late."

Caulder's eyes softened, and he smiled slightly. "Yeah," he said, "we can. It's never really too late to build something. And Christy can be part of it, too, at least part-time. I made the mistake of thinking that since she was a girl, her mom should raise her. I cheated her out of a lot, and she knows it. I feel it sometimes when we're together. I owe your sister."

• • •

Stacy walked into her dining room and slid into her seat beside Ryan, who sat in his high chair, eating the raspberry jam off the face of his toast. She put a hand out and caught his arm as he was about to turn the toast into a Frisbee, took it from him, and put it on her own plate. Her father was a late sleeper and would not be up this morning until long after Stacy had left for school, but her mother sat before a full breakfast of eggs and bacon and toast. She was a big, strong, round woman with energy enough to power the entire family, and she looked entirely capable of taking on surrogate motherhood at this late age of sixty-one. She had accepted Stacy's pregnancy out of hand, with never a word of judgment or hint of rebuke. Stacy's father had not been capable of quite so grand an acceptance of events but through his wife's sheer will had been forced to accept not only the relationship with Preston as he watched it disintegrate into a narcotic fog over the months but the fact that Stacy would carry Preston's baby to term and would refuse to give it up for adoption. Early on a serious rift had developed between Stacy and her dad over the situation, but time and relentless good-humored pushing by Mrs. Ryder had helped both Stacy and her father overcome it.

Stacy lifted the lid over the frying pan and removed

two poached eggs, skipped the bacon, and dropped two pieces of toast into the toaster. "I'm going to tell," she said to her mother seated in the dining room. "Today."

"Tell what, dear?"

"Who the drool king really belongs to," Stacy said, moving to the doorway to catch her mother's reaction, but Isabelle Ryder prided herself in never giving away startled inner responses.

"Really," she said. "Why would you want to do that?"

"The longer I put it off," Stacy said, "the more I'll look like a fool when people find out. If it was a mistake, it's mine, and I may as well start living with it." Stacy had been awake most of the night, running the dialogue at Jackie's over and over. There was more than what she'd heard, she was sure of that; Jennifer Lawless had been too pulled back, too reserved to be responding merely to Dillon's revelations about Preston. But all that aside, Dillon had made a valiant effort to get to the truth of the world as he knew it, and Stacy appreciated that. Dillon had a certain dignity when he went off half cocked. That was the thing she had always missed in Preston: the ability to shoot from the hip while pretending you had taken great care to aim. As she had knelt next to Ryan's crib following her second visit to his room that night to comfort him, she realized what was missing in her life. It wasn't Preston—he'd been gone long before he was gone—it was humor. It was laughter. She remembered when, not so long ago, she had been joyful most of the time. That's why she had always been such good friends with Dillon; he made her laugh. Preston owned her heart, but Dillon had laid claim to her spirit long ago. Since Preston's death—since that bastard *killed himself*—there had been no more joy. And without the joy she had wedged Dillon out. Dillon was the Good Humor man, and she knew she had been turning away from him and all he stood for since the funeral. And since the baby—since the *shame*—there had been even less. What Stacy understood, kneeling there in the moonglow, gazing at Ryan—as joyful a creator of human waste as toddled the face of the earth—was that she didn't *really feel* any of the shame, and she didn't feel the sadness of Preston anymore either. She played at feeling those things because that's what people—her parents included—expected. Peering through the wooden bars at Ryan, his fist crammed halfway down his throat, looking for all the world as if he were guzzling the contents of his arm, Stacy Ryder called a halt to her time of mourning. And she also called a halt to her time of lies. You can't laugh when you lie because lies signify shame, and there is no laughter in shame.

No more.

"I'm not sure that's a good idea, dear," Mrs. Ryder said now. "Maybe we should talk about it."

Stacy shook her head. "There's nothing more to talk about. I'm tired of everyone at school treating me like some kind of saint for helping my parents out in this 'time of crisis.' That's what Mr. Caldwell called it the other day. A 'time of crisis.' I'm like some kind of tragic heroine or something."

"There are worse things," her mother said.

"Like having people know you slept with a drug addict and he probably killed himself because you told him you were pregnant?"

Mrs. Ryder put her fingers to her temples, massaging them gently. Her job in this family was to still the waters, keep an even keel. That wasn't always easy, but her presentation of calm in any storm was a powerful tool in that regard. "There's more to it than that, Stacy. We've talked about this."

Stacy sat next to Ryan with her breakfast. She hadn't expected her mother's blessing, merely felt she should let her know before carrying out her plan. "Well, anyway," she said, "that's what I'm thinking. You and Dad going anywhere this weekend?"

What Dillon loved about Stacy Ryder as much as anything was her capriciousness. From the time they were small children she delighted—and sometimes horrified—him with her off-the-wall actions, seemingly performed without the slightest regard for the consequences. Years back at the traveling carnival, after she had slipped those Chinese handcuffs over his finger, allowing his sister to escape into the crowd, she had given no thought whatever to the harassment Dillon would face when his mother caught up to him, which as he remembered, was substantial. Even back before that, in first grade, she had pulled off an impulsive move so cold-blooded even Dillon began to fear her. On a day in December that started out below zero Fahrenheit and seemed to get colder, the kids spent morning recess indoors, playing games and coloring. Stacy and a kid named Johnny McMasters got into a squabble over who was going to use the *yellow* first, and Stacy won out, having by far the better grip. Johnny evened the score a few minutes later with a hard shot between the shoulder blades, and before Stacy could lay waste to him, the teacher stepped in and stopped it.

During afternoon recess, when the temperature had finally crawled a little closer to zero, several of the more hearty students bundled up and went out onto the playground with the teacher's aide, and Stacy challenged them all to follow the leader through a little obstacle course she had set up, which ended with a rung-by-rung trip across the playground high bars. Stacy made it all the way across, a substantial feat for a first grader whose grip was eroded considerably from the thick wool mittens covering her hands, but most of the rest of the kids fell to the snow after the first or second rung. Dillon made it all the way, and Johnny McMasters, a sinewy little whippet with tenacity to match his revenge quotient, was now about halfway but losing his grip.

"Hold on," Stacy yelled. "Just rest a minute. You can make it."

Johnny, having forgotten the morning fracas, listened intently. "I'm slipping," he grunted. "My hands are slipping."

Stacy stood directly below him. "Try to pull yourself up," she said. "Slip your elbows over the rungs. Then you can rest while you hang there."

Dillon saw a look pass over Stacy's face as she coaxed Johnny on. He wondered why she was helping her earlier assailant, knowing from personal experience that was definitely not Stacy-like.

Miraculously, and with a little help from Stacy pushing up on his feet, Johnny pulled himself up far enough to slide his arm over the rung and support himself by the crook of his elbow, then follow suit with his other arm. He dangled there at the center of the rungs, adjusting his mittens and resting his hands to continue the journey.

"Wanna do something neat?" Stacy asked from below.

"What?" Johnny yelled back.

"Put your tongue on the bar."

"What?"

"Put your tongue on the bar. It's like a Popsicle."

Johnny stuck out his tongue, which was instantly welded to the freezing bar.

Stacy turned and walked toward the school, where the teacher's aide was calling them all in.

Dillon was caught—wide eyed—between walking back to the teacher with Stacy, which he wanted to do, and trying to help Johnny, who could soon be hanging by the tongue, screaming bloody murder. He chose the former but halfway across the playground stopped and said, "Stace. We can't just leave him."

Stacy turned around and yelled back, as loud as she could, "Just let go and drop, you big baby."

Mr. and Mrs. Ryder spent some after-school conference time for *that* one. The teacher's aide was so angry she saved the piece of skin left stuck to the frozen bar and presented it to them when they came to get Stacy, and it was a *long* time before anyone played with *her* after school or on weekends. She at least tied the Guinness world record for time grounded by a child under prison age. But she was adamant through it all that circumstances being the same, she'd do it again, exactly the same.

Not only was she capricious, but she stuck by her impulses.

Stacy walked into the school office and stood quietly behind Linda Moore, the first-period student office aide, who read the morning bulletin over the intercom to the homeroom classes. Stacy waited patiently, glancing down at the prepared speech she had written in case she got the jitters and couldn't remember what she wanted to say.

"Preliminary cheerleader tryouts for next year will be held in the gym immediately after school on Friday," Linda read. "Single male teachers wishing to apply for judgeships should meet Mr. Caldwell behind the school at noon today. Bring money."

What a throwback, Stacy thought. *I wonder how long it'll be before the National Organization for Women finds a terrorist to come take him out.*

"And finally," Linda read on, "there will be a pep assembly in the gym Friday morning to help spur the girls' hoopsters through the district tournament, which begins Friday night out at Three Forks Community College. Bring noise." Linda reached to flip the mike off, but Stacy touched her shoulder.

"Mr. Caldwell wants me to read this," she said, and Linda stepped away from the mike.

Stacy took a deep breath and scanned the written copy in her hand, crumpled it, and put her mouth next to the mike. "One last-minute announcement," she said.

Dillon sat in his homeroom, reading a book called *The Ultimate Athlete* that had been recommended by Coach. A lot of it seemed aerie fairie and "Twilight Zone"-ish, but Coach had told him it was worth it to read through all that to get to some exceptional concentration techniques. Even if he were too closed-minded to accept the concepts, she said, challenging him as usual, he could get some good out of the concrete exercises, ones especially relevant for long-distance runners and swimmers and the like. Especially good for Ironmen, Coach had said.

His head snapped up when he heard Stacy's voice, and he reached back to the seat behind him and tapped Jennifer on the arm. "Isn't that Stace?"

"This is Stacy Ryder," the voice over the intercom said, "and I bring news of a hoax that has been perpetrated upon you."

Dillon squeezed Jennifer's arm and gritted his teeth. "I think I'm about to become an uncle."

"Most of you who know me," Stacy went on, "know my parents recently adopted a baby because our relatives, the baby's supposed parents, couldn't care for it. Well, there was no adoption. No careless South Dakota cousin and no twilight-years parenthood for my folks. The kid is mine. Signed, sealed, and painfully delivered. His daddy was a drug addict, but he's got a class set of grandparents on both sides, so I think he has a pretty good chance. If you see Dillon Hemingway in the halls today, you might want to congratulate him on his uncleship. And by the way, Dillon, if you haven't been given another three-day vacation and you're out there in intercom land, you best hurry your butt to the phone and tell your poppa so he doesn't have to get the news from some overzealous administrator.

"Thanks, Linda. How do you turn this thing off?" floated over the intercom as, back in the office, Stacy turned away from the intercom. Linda reached over and flipped the switch, then stood staring at Stacy.

Stacy shrugged.

Linda said, "Did Mr. Caldwell really want you to read that?"

Stacy shrugged again.

"That took guts."

"The truth will set me free, right?" Stacy said. She turned and walked out the door toward her first-period class.

CHAPTER 12

Dear Preston,

Well, the big wheel keeps on turnin'—and gathering speed. I keep going back to what Coach said about responses and all, and I figure it's pretty easy coming up with wisdom while you're hanging out in her office shootin' the crap and folding clothes, but it's another thing altogether to *act* in any kind of "right" way, if there is such a thing.

I can't get Jen and her stepdad out of my head. I've tried everything. I've tried to run it out, swim it out, drown it out with MTV; but nothing helps, and nothing changes it. I think I said before I've got a motion picture brain, and I just keep seeing it over and over.

I tried to find out what I can do about it, but without being able to say anything specific, it's hard to get information. I called Child Protective Services, but the lady there said she couldn't help me unless I was willing to give names and some details. She did say if I don't want to report it myself, I could tell a teacher or counselor or administrator at school, that they were legally required to report child abuse or neglect. That didn't help me as much as it hurt me because if I were going to go for advice, it would be to Coach, but if I do that, she would be under the gun to call it in. The fine for failure to report is ten thousand dollars, so Coach could be out some serious summer vacation money.

And then there's the part about sticking my nose in other people's business, a practice you mentioned a time or two if I remember right. Jen was crystal clear she didn't want me messing in this at all. Since she tried to get help before and got only trouble, I'm the only person she's told. If I tell, my trust is down the toilet. I have to trust her to know what's best for her; I mean, she's been there. And I know how I feel when someone gets into *my* stuff uninvited. On the other hand, this isn't the same as someone spying on my training schedule or starting rumors about who I like or don't like. It isn't even the same as people sticking their noses into my private stuff about you. This is ongoing. It's ongoing, and it's uglier than anything I can think of. For me, it's like knowing my best friend is standing knee-deep in a nest of rattlesnakes and I'm just watching her be poisoned. Actually it's more like knowing how bad things were for you and not being able to do anything about it.

So everyplace I've turned there's been a block. I went back to Jen, and she simply wouldn't discuss it anymore. I can't tell Stacy because you *know* she'd go off and do something to Jen's stepdad—like make him stick his tongue on a freezing playground bar.

Maybe not his tongue . . .

Dad would want to go the rational way, which is through the law, and so would Coach. Truth is, I'd go along with any of those things if I could just know I was not making things worse, that Jen wouldn't go right down the same road she's been down before.

So I figured since Caldwell has been so generous to me with all the three-day vacations, I should take one on my own, give him a rest. Actually I took only one day—told Dad I was sick this morning, waited for him to head out to work, hopped into your van, and drove to St. Mary's College out there on the river. There's a guy in their psychology department who's supposed to be one of the leading authorities in the Northwest on child abuse and particularly on sexual victims and offenders. He's semifamous and has been on TV and radio around here fairly regularly for the past two years, usually when there's a series of rapes or other outlandish sexual shenanigans that the cops need help with, so it was no big detective deal for me to figure out he might be able to help.

I must be living right because when I walked into the outer offices of the psych department and asked to see him, the secretary rang his number, and he was out to greet me in seconds, without even knowing why I was there. I knew he was probably in the same reporting position as Coach, and I wanted to keep it abstract, so I started to go with some theoretical bullshit, like I was writing a research paper or something, but it was a stupid lie I knew I couldn't hold, and I gave it up quick.

"Actually," I said, starting anew, "I have a friend, and her stepdad is messing with her. I promised I wouldn't give her name or anything, or tell anyone, but it's driving me nuts."

He invited me into his office, and I was instantly comfortable with him. His name is Dr. Newcomb, and there is nothing physically outstanding about him other than the way he dresses. He wears glasses, he's of medium height and weight and coloring, and he wears the clothes you'd expect him to wear—a jacket and slacks—but they look like he picked them up off the stairs on his way out the door. I mean, they look like he sends them out to get them wrinkled.

Anyway, he motioned for me to sit down. "She needs to tell someone," he said. "That's the only way things like this get stopped."

I gave him the whole story—without names, of course—about how he was a bigwig who couldn't be touched, how Jen had tried once before and made her life all the more miserable. Dr. Newcomb asked a lot of questions, some of which I knew the answers to and others that I didn't, so when I stopped talking, I figured he knew as much about it as anyone. I sort of expected him to give me the standard line about how if no one steps forward, there's no way to help and all that, but he didn't.

He said, "That's the trouble with the protection system sometimes. Everyone who works in it is backed up to last year. A good lawyer can go in and turn things upside down, and the state can't afford the time or energy to take him on. I hate to say it, but this system doesn't protect rich kids the way it does poor kids."

"So what can I do?"

"You probably can't do anything. Your friend has to be willing to do something, including take this guy on. I hate to say it, but you're probably smart not to report it. CPS would investigate, but if the lawyer made enough noise or the girl backed down even a little, they'd close it. Then she's stuck holding the bag. And the way you describe him, this guy sounds mean. And dangerous."

"Actually, that's not my description," I said. "It's hers."

Dr. Newcomb nodded. "Tell you what I can offer," he said. "If you can get her to come see me, and I'm convinced she's telling the truth, I'll go after him myself. I'm considered the expert in this town, so I have a little more clout than a lot of folks. See if you can at least get her to talk. She doesn't have to give me her last name unless she wants to; that way I can't report it if she doesn't feel safe."

That was as good news as I'd heard since Jen told me about this nightmare. I knew she'd be mad as hell at me for getting into it at all, but if she could get past that, there might be a chance. I thanked the doctor and got up to leave.

"There are a few things you should know if this is your girl friend," he said.

I stopped. "She is. Sort of. I want her to be, I think."

He nodded. "I'll bet it's been confusing."

"It's been confusing."

"You need to know that she sees relationships very differently from other people, particularly if there's anything remotely sexual about them. She's spent her life being invaded—unable to protect her body, that one part of her most of us have control over. I could go into all kinds of detail about the confusion she has and her complete lack of trust, but it would be too much for you to take in. What I will say is, if the two of you ever decide to have a real relationship, don't try to do it without help. You can't repair that kind of damage without a lot of therapy."

Boy, that's what I needed to hear, Pres. I needed to hear that even if this all does work out, I could still be in for the screwball love affair of the decade. God, I'm sending away for a blow-up doll. I told him that. Except for the part about the doll.

"Believe it," he said, and he leveled his eyes on mine, and I almost thought I felt a push from inside. Whatever it was, it was powerful. "Believe it."

I nodded. "I do believe it. Thanks."

I started on out the door, but turned back out of curiosity. "What makes a guy do things like this?" I asked. "I mean, something must have happened to him. . . ."

Dr. Newcomb put his hand in the air. "I'm sure his childhood was filled with monstrous acts against him, Dillon," he said, "but don't even think about it. When a dog turns rabid it doesn't do you a bit of good to think about when he was a puppy. That's *my* job, not yours."

I plan to hit Jen with all that, but not right now. It helps me to know there might be a way out of all this, so that quiets the beasts in my head, but the district tournament starts tonight, and if I brought up something with even the remotest possibility of screwing up her concentration on that, she'd rip out my innards and dine on them.

Stacy bowled over the troops the other day, announced her motherhood during homeroom bulletin and let the chips fall where they may, as they say. You're famous once again, little big brother. The world now knows you live on. · She got a few looks in the hallowed halls, but everyone who said anything supported her. I think people do have some inner respect for the truth, even if it's about hard things— things they don't like to look at. They may not always agree with it, and they may not really want to hear it, but when you tell it and stand by it big and strong, not many will mess with it. Maybe that's a good thing about humans. Quick! Write it down.

I need to get over to the community college and get ready for the game. We actually have a pretty easy draw tonight. Since we finished on top of our league, we get the weakest team from the Southeast District, which is Pasco. But you never know. They're at least good enough to be there, so they aren't pushovers. Coach isn't about to let her team look past a game. It's single elimination, so you get only one chance to screw up. My pregame job is taping, rubdowns, and hype, so I need to get all the rest of this crap out of my head and focus on something I can do something about. I know how much you want to spend your first years in the afterlife reading about sports at Chief Joseph High School, so I'm outta here.

                    Dillon

CHAPTER 13

Dedicated fans began filing into the Three Forks Community College gymnasium more than an hour ahead of the scheduled starting time for the first game of the girls' triple-A high school District IV tournament. Dillon was already busy in the locker room, taping ankles and knees, preparing to work on specific muscle complaints of the girls who lined up for massages. Dillon believed the big games were as important to him as to the players; he felt as much a part of the team as any of them. The girls respected him not only because of his paramedical expertise, which was quite advanced for a high school student, but for the fact that he knew firsthand the pain and pleasure of athletic discipline. Besides that, most of them thought he was cute and funny.

Jennifer sat in the corner, fully dressed in her uniform and warm-up, a towel pulled low over her face, concentrating on the upcoming game. Chief Joe had drawn Rogers High School for the first game, and though the matchup had the potential for a rout, there was no room for arrogance. The regional tournament was single elimination: Lose one and you're out. Go directly to jail. Do not pass Go. Do not get a shot at the state title.

Dillon glanced over at Jen and mentally assessed whether or not he should interrupt her. Despite the fact that she seemed locked in her concentration, he moved over and squatted in front of her. "How's the hamstring?"

Jen jumped, looking for an instant as if he were a complete stranger, then nodded. "Okay, I think. You might help me stretch a little."

"How you feelin'?" he asked, but she put up her hand and shook her head, his signal not to talk but to take care of business. Dillon nodded, and Jen rolled over onto her stomach so he could apply gentle pressure to her upper hamstring with the heels of both hands. He felt the leg relax under the pressure and firmly, but still gently, applied more. He took the leg through some more stretches, ones Jen couldn't do herself, and told her how to keep it warm. Just before the game he would wrap it with a little heat to keep it loose. Jen nodded in acknowledgment and went back into her pregame world while Dillon moved about the other girls, taking care of their aches and pains and teasing a little to loosen them up, though this was a team with lots of big-game experience and not at all likely to choke under pressure.

Coach Sherman moved through the locker room, talking with individual players about their assignments, quizzing each about the Rogers player who was likely to be her opponent. She believed it was important to know not only the opposing team's offense but as much about each player running it as possible. Same with defense. Seldom were any of Coach Sherman's players surprised by another player's abilities.

Minutes before time to hit the floor for warm-ups Coach called them all to circle around her and summarized Chief Joe's general game plan once again. "We're coming out fast," she said. "If they want to stay with us, they'll have to prove it from the gun. Full-court pressure, work the fast break. Man-to-man defense all the way." She quickly outlined on the chalkboard two of the newer offenses they had worked on for the past three weeks, called for questions, and, when there were none, sent the girls charging onto the floor.

She caught Dillon at the dressing room door. "What's with Jen?" she asked.

"What do you mean?"

"She seems pretty far gone. More than usual. I don't know, maybe it's my imagination."

Dillon reflected on the past few moments. Coach was right, Jen had been encased in stainless steel, but nothing about her surprised him anymore. He smiled and shrugged. "Game face, is all. I think. Wouldn't want to be Rogers tonight, I know that."

"Dillon, is something going on with her that you're not talking about? She's been different for the past week or so. If anyone would know, you would."

Dillon was caught off guard and sputtered a little but caught himself. "I don't think so," he lied. "I mean, she hasn't said anything. Might be, though, if it feels that way to you. You're not wrong much."

On the court Jen worked through the warm-up drills as if it were the last three minutes of the fourth quarter and Chief Joe were down by five. Her moves to the hoop were strong and hard, her jump shot on the money. In the three-on-three defensive drills her teammates couldn't get a shot off against her unless they backed way out of range.

Coach Sherman walked among the players, giving them little tips and lots of encouragement, keeping things loose and doing that last little bit of fine tuning that was probably more for her than it was for the girls.

The captains met at mid-court, and Jen listened to the referees' instructions impassively, absently watching the stands fill to near capacity. The opposing bands and cheerleading squads were working the crowd to a fevered pitch. Normally Jen loved that; it worked directly into her own psych-up, but tonight she simply stared as the referee talked, reaching up to slap the hands of the Rogers cocaptains when he'd finished.

She walked back to the huddle to tell Coach and the rest of the team that Rogers was meat, then shed her warm-ups as Coach gave last-minute instructions. The players joined hands, shouting their chant, then took the floor.

From the opening inbounds pass the game belonged to Chief Joseph. Jennifer blocked the first two shots her man took and scored six points before Rogers could work up a sweat: four on quick jumpers and two on a drive to the hoop that left her defender standing and reaching. The girl couldn't get close enough even to foul. Her teammates rose to her intensity and by the time Rogers was able to call its first time-out, Chief Joe was up 11–2 and high as kites. Coach Sherman quickly outlined a press break to counter the full-court press Rogers would surely come out in. "I wouldn't worry about it too much, though. You keep playing like you're playing and they're going to need a hell of a lot more than a press. They can't press you if they can't catch you. Okay, take it to 'em. Lookin' great, Jen."

Jen stared at the floor, looked up quickly, and nodded. Back out on the court she took up where she had left off. Rogers trapped Chief Joe's point guard, and Jen came back to help, taking the pass and dribbling through the press, then firing a pinpoint pass to the center, breaking down the key for the easy lay-up. Before the ball was through the net, Jen was back at the half line, stalking her man with relentless ferocity. Chief Joe's defense was so effective that the thirty-second shot clock ran to five before Rogers could get any kind of decent pass into the key, but when it finally came into its weak side forward, she beat her man and drove to the hoop, cutting behind a screen set on Jen and pushing strong to the basket. Jen spun off the screen and, with a second left on the shot clock, sprang from behind, clamping her hand over the ball and driving both ball and shooter to the hardwood. The block was absolutely clean, and as the ball rolled into the hands of Chief Joe's shooting guard and the Chief Joe crowd leaped to its collective feet, Jen sprinted for the opposite end.

And kept right on going.

Dillon sat awed by Jennifer's defensive move. He saw it from behind and to the side, saw daylight between the bodies and Jen's big, powerful hand close over the leather, forcing the Rogers forward to the ground, saw her lat muscle and tricep flex tight as she twisted like a ballet dancer to avoid the contact. He leaped spontaneously to his feet with the rest of the crowd, wishing at once this were television so he could see the instant replay. He followed the ball downcourt in the hands of Lila Sprague, the shooting guard who retrieved it, and his brain took an instant to compute what he saw out of the corner of his eye: Jennifer running all the way to the baseline, then on out the door. The cheers shifted to a loud murmur, and he looked down the bench to Coach, who could only look back puzzled. For an instant Dillon thought Jen had run to the locker room, maybe with an injury, but quickly realized the only thing out the end doors was outdoors.

Coach Sherman called time simultaneously with the blast of the referee's whistle, and by then Dillon realized something was really wrong. "I'll get her!" he yelled at

Coach. "Go on with the game," and he sprinted for the door, almost bowling over the refs, who conferenced quickly to decide whether there was a technical foul here or what.

Outside, Dillon stopped a second to let his eyes adjust to the dark, then darted down the only path Jen could have taken, across the treelined lawn toward the entrance of campus and out to the street. Toward the end of the path, by the administration building, he thought he saw a shadow flash across an opening. If it was Jen, she was *moving*.

He shot down the path, getting good purchase with his running shoes on the frozen snow; Dillon always wore his sweats and runners to games because he often ran home for training. He sprinted the seventy-five yards down the snowy path to the street and glanced quickly both ways. Initially he saw nothing, and his mind raced out of control. *What could she be doing? Where? Toward town? Toward the bridge?* His heart froze. The bridge. At its highest point it was easily four hundred feet above the river. *For Jen to run out of a basketball game . . .* He couldn't think it, just tightened down a steel clamp on his mind and raced in the direction of the bridge, knowing full well now she had gone that way. It was less than a mile, and she probably had a hundred-yard lead. She was fast. Dillon was faster, but had no idea whether he could overtake her in that short a distance.

He pushed hard, just under a sprint, and occasionally caught her shadow passing under a streetlamp up ahead. He glimpsed her twice and knew he was gaining. He picked up his pace. The cold air seared his lungs, and a familiar burning began in his thighs. He blocked out his awful fear and concentrated on speed. His rhythmic breathing became labored, and he realized he was running too fast to hold the pace, but he couldn't slow down for fear of being a second too slow. Once again he visualized the triangle, placing it in its familiar spot at the back of his skull, and gathered the pain throughout his body, placing its fiery red imprint into the confines of the three thick borders, where he could manage it, or at least tolerate it. His speed increased. *Going for a photo finish,* he thought. *Neck and neck with Jen's asshole stepdad.*

Now he could see her the whole way and thought to yell, but feared she might panic. She couldn't know he was there, and he didn't want to give her reason to run faster. And he didn't have the wind.

When Jen reached the entrance to the bridge, Dillon had closed to within ten yards. The slope below was gradual, and if Jennifer were going to jump, she would have to make it at least halfway across to get the height she needed to do the job right. Miraculously, she hadn't heard Dillon closing in over her own heavy breathing and sobs. He might get only one chance.

Jen ran close to the edge now. There was a short suicide fence to climb, but she knew she could make it over.

She heard Dillon too late, as he dived for her feet. He wrapped her legs in a perfect downfield tackle, and they fell on the packed snow in a heap. In an instant she was kicking his head, scrambling away, screaming, "Get away from me! Get away from me!"

"No way!" He gasped. "What the hell's the matter with you?"

She kicked his head again and scrambled up. "Get away from me, you bastard!"

Dillon's head reeled as Jen struggled away and sprinted for the center of the span. He caught her again, but his tackle was less than picture perfect this time, and Jennifer kicked him square in the temple.

He pulled himself to his feet again as his head cleared in time to see her sprinting on across the bridge. His temples pounded. A nauseating dizziness danced between his head and stomach, and his steps became less sure. Jen was just a few yards ahead, but Dillon could only keep her pace; he could not close on her.

At the end of the bridge Jen cut left and aimed down the steep embankment toward the river and the trail running alongside it, back toward the regional park. Dillon followed but tripped in the darkness on a rock, pitching head over heels to the bottom of the hill. Jen raced along the path, knowing she had gained ground because she could no longer hear him. Dillon picked himself up and immediately dropped to the ground in electric pain, his ankle throbbing and stabbing him from within. He felt the swelling, and he reached down to tighten his laces, hoping to create a partial cast enough to keep up the chase. Jen was serious, no doubt about it. If he didn't catch her, she'd be dead in minutes. He didn't know how, but he knew she'd do it.

The pain in his foot throbbed almost unbearably, but Dillon was not about to have this repeat performance in his life, and he gathered it, stuffing it into the triangle in the back of his brain, and pushed on down the dark path.

Jen stopped as she spotted the water tower looming easily a hundred and fifty feet in the air, like a monolith in the center of the flat, snowy clearing. The ladder didn't reach the ground, but she had gone up there many times as a child to be alone, leaning a picnic table against the side to reach the bottom rung. She glanced back to see Dillon coming. Once again her best friend was her worst enemy. Quickly she dragged the table the few feet across the snow, leaned it diagonally against the huge tank, stood back, and ran, springing from the table to the bottom rung. She climbed quickly, oblivious to the bitter cold against her skin, her hands nearly numb.

Having watched Jen's method for reaching the ladder, Dillon played follow the leader, stumbling across the snow to the table on his severely sprained ankle. His ankle gave way when it hit the tabletop, sending him tumbling in agony back into the snow. He was up in a flash. This time he pushed off his good foot, barely catching hold of the frozen bottom rung, pulling himself up with only the strength in his arms. A shocking pain shot through his foot at every rung, but he used his other foot and his powerful arms to pull himself up the ladder at almost twice Jen's pace, and he could see himself closing.

Jen could see nothing. Blinded by semifrozen tears, she climbed, intent only on keeping her grip on the frozen rungs. She knew Dillon was behind her and pushed hard toward the top, unaware she was screaming at her mother with every step, and at T.B. Her voice echoed across the park, and Dillon was surprised that he strained to hear her words. A mixture of desperation and rage burned through him. He would condemn her to hell if she jumped.

Jen reached the catwalk stretching across the top of the tower and followed the accompanying rail toward the opposite edge as Dillon pulled himself over the last rung. She reached the end of the catwalk, blocked from her final quest by only three steel rails. Closing her eyes, she dropped to slide under and end it. Dillon's hand clamped around her wrist in a vise lock.

"Let me go!" she screamed in surprise. "Let me go, you bastard!"

He held tight, too exhausted even to answer, straining to tow her back.

"Let me go!" she screamed again, and, with another violent kick, nailed him in the teeth. Again his grip weakened as his head exploded and his mouth filled with the salty taste of blood. Jen slid nearly out of his grasp and on under the rail as he lunged, catching the back of her basketball shorts, pulling himself close enough to wrap one arm around her chest and under her arm at the moment she let go. He locked his injured foot onto the rail and grasped it with his free hand, again forcing out the searing pain.

Intent only on prying herself loose, Jennifer Lawless dangled a hundred and fifty feet above the icy ground.

"Let me go!" she screamed again. "Let me go! It's my life, you asshole! Let me go!"

"No" was all he could manage. His grip was secure, and at that moment he felt strong enough to hold it forever.

"What happened?" he yelled at her. "Tell me what happened!"

"Let me go!" she screamed again.

Deep, appalling, dreadful pain welled up in his chest, almost paralyzing pain, as he realized the consequences to himself if he let her go. "Jen, if you go, I go."

"No!" she screamed. "This is mine! God damn you, Dillon. God damn you!"

"I can't do this again!" he screamed back. "Not again! I'm not letting go. If you go, I go."

"You bastard!" Jen screamed. "You bastard! Let me go!"

"Think of your sister!" he yelled. "What's she gonna do? Who's going to stop your son-of-a-bitching stepdad from going after her? Answer me that! Who's going to stop him?"

Jen started to sob. Dillon felt her body go limp, the fight gone.

"Come on," Dillon said. "Come on back up. We can do something." He tried to hoist her back but didn't have strength or leverage enough to get her through the bottom rails. Jen hung limp. "You gotta help me, Jen. Help me. Climb up my arm. Please!"

Still she sobbed.

"We'll do something, Jen. Really we will. You gotta help me. If you go, I go. I can't be here for another one. Please, help me."

Between them, they worked Jennifer far enough back up to where she caught the rail and pulled herself up, collapsing on the cold metal catwalk. Dillon held her, removed his warm-up top, and wrapped it around her shoulders as she heaved and convulsed in sobs. Neither was aware they could very well be freezing to death.

When her body finally slackened, he said, "What happened?"

"My mother," she choked out.

"What?"

"She came home today, just before I was ready to leave for the game. All smiles and giggly, like a little kid with 'great news' for us." Jen started to cry again. "She's pregnant. That bitch is pregnant. She'd just come back from an ultrasound. My goddamn mother is pregnant. And it's a girl."

The implications bloomed full in Dillon's mind.

"I had convinced Dawn to leave with me," Jen said. "I finally figured out I have to leave Mom there. If she wants out, she'll have to do it herself. But now she's pregnant. And it's a girl. She waited for the ultrasound to tell us, wanted to be sure the baby was okay. It's a girl. It's okay. It's okay until the minute it gets here. Then it gets *my* life. I can't do it, Dillon. I can get Dawn out, but now there's a baby. A baby girl. I can't beat him, Dillon. He'll kill it. He'll kill its heart, just like he did mine."

"We'll do something," Dillon said. "I promise we'll do something. It'll work. I talked to a guy. There are some things we can do. Really there are. If not, we'll just steal her. We'll steal her and go. I promise, Jen. We will. We'll do something."

Jen looked up at him, and for the first time she gave herself over. "Will you? Will you help me? Someone's got to, Dillon. I can't go on like this."

"I'll help," he said. "Now let's get out of here."

CHAPTER 14

Dear Preston,

So much for the Ironman for a while. Three Forks, Washington's favorite renegade triathlete is out of commission. Got me an ankle like a medium-size mushmelon and some serious dental considerations. The ankle is worse. Doc says I'd have been better off to have broken it. Instead, I tore all the ligaments and rendered it as useless as an appendix or tonsils. It's going to be a good six months before I can do any serious running, though I'll be able to get into the water before that, and I should be able to do some stationary biking with my other leg if I use a stirrup. Maybe this is a little bit of what you felt like. No. That's like saying I did *Black Like Me* by wearing black shoe polish under my arms. Anyway, I should be able to hit a couple of late-summer or early-fall triathlons, though I

certainly won't be at my best. But for now, I'm keeping my
ankle above heart level and an ice bag on my lip—over the
hole where my left front tooth used to be. Jen kicked that
sucker clean out, trying to kill her goddamn self. She been
talking to you? She tried to jump off the old water tower
down in the regional park, the one you and I used to try to
figure out how to get on top of. Ran right out in the middle
of a basketball game out at the community college, with
me on her tail, only she didn't know it. This was not what
the professionals call an adolescent vie for attention. This
was serious shit. She beat me half to death, trying to get to
do it. I'm glad she didn't have your Luger.

I found out some things about myself that night, Pres: I
got a good look at my physical limits. When the stakes are
high enough, I can take a *lot*. And I learned something
about stakes. If I'd lost her, if I couldn't have pulled her
back, then I really think I'd have gone with her. I can't have
another suicide. Not on my watch. It's just too ugly, leaves
me with way too much that can't be fixed and too much hate
for myself—too much wondering what I could have done,
what I should have seen coming. If life is important, then
god damn it, it's important, and people have to do everything
they can to keep it going when they get the chance. Their
own or anyone else's. And it must be important or everyone
wouldn't be making such a big deal about it. I guess it

doesn't do a whole lot of good telling you that.

Telling a big enough lie to cover the events of that night hasn't been all that easy, and it's way too much to hope anybody believes it. I mean, Jennifer Lawless ran out in the middle of a basketball game, and it wasn't *just* a basketball game, it was a *tournament* game, and it wasn't just a tournament game, it was a tournament game she was winning almost single-handedly. I want to tell you before she split, she was kicking *butt*.

We didn't go back to the gym. Both of us were freezing, and I could barely walk, and I couldn't think of a good enough explanation so Jen could just walk back in out of the cold and take up in the fourth quarter where she'd left off in the first. Besides, even if I had been *Papa* Hemingway and able to concoct such a story, Jen wasn't interested. So we went to our place—Dad was out of town for the weekend at Uncle Brad's in Seattle—and made some hot chocolate and called Coach's answering machine and left a message for her to call when she got back. Then I gave Jen some gym shorts and a tank top and got a dry swimsuit for myself, and we hopped into the bathtub, which Dad has turned into one of those two-seat Jacuzzis, and we cranked up the heat while I iced my ankle out over the edge, and somehow we got our body temperatures back above the hypothermia level.

So I said, "How come you tried to kill yourself and I'm the one that's almost dead?"

Jen didn't answer. You suicidal types don't have all that great a sense of humor, you know that? I remembered back on the water tower Jen had told me what set all this off was she found out her mother was pregnant and it was a girl. They tested, I guess because she's old, and they wanted to make sure the baby's okay. Jen is sure that this new kid'll have the same kind of life she has if she's going to be raised by T.B. I told her back there that we'd do something. In fact, I said if we had to, we'd steal the baby when it's born.

I put my arms around Jen and pulled her back against me, and she didn't resist. "I wasn't just hollering to keep you from jumping back there," I said. "We'll do something. This has all gone way too far." I went on to tell her some of my conversation with Dr. Newcomb, the psych guy I told you about in the last letter, and she at least listened this time, didn't stand on her idea that nothing would work. Maybe she was just too tired.

"Tell me what you want to do when Coach calls," I said.

She said, "I want to pretend we're not here."

"We can't do that. Not to Coach. She's got to be worried sick."

"I know," Jen said. "But that's what I *want* to do. Tell her I'm okay and I'll talk to her tomorrow. Before the game." She took a deep breath. "I don't know what to do. I can't tell the team what's going on, and if anyone finds out what really happened, I'll end up in the psych wing at Sacred Heart."

I know it sounds selfish to think about my own position in all this, what with Jen a heartbeat away from joining you in Teenager Heaven and a district basketball championship hanging in the balance and that asshole T.B. on the loose in the world, but I'm in a tough spot. This is *suicide* we're dealing with, and I'm in *no way* competent to deal with that. I proved that conclusively once before, don't you think? I fix injuries and fine-tune bodies, not psychos. But the pros have had a go at this one, and all they do is mess it up. I lay awake all that night thinking. Part of me knew this is way too big for me to handle alone, but another part knew I could push Jen right over the edge by telling the wrong people. Everything I do has to be protected, and the people who could help me the most were the people who could mess it up the worst—Coach and Dad. But the alternative, like I said, was to try to handle it myself, and like I said, I'm a *body* man.

I realized something else. I know the distance I'm willing to stick my neck out has vastly increased because when I was on top of that water tower and I really thought I might be going over if I couldn't get her to help me pull her back, my commitment to stop all this expanded exponentially. Crazy as it sounded, I didn't rule out killing him. And I wouldn't do it like the kids who've tried so far—doing the deed, then throwing themselves on the mercy of society and the courts. No way, Red Ryder. If I did it, no one would know. When I thought of it up there on the tower, no one in the world except Jen even knew I have a reason to hate him. The few times I've even spoken with him have been civil as the day is long. I didn't like thinking about that too much, though, unless I couldn't find any other way, 'cause I gotta tell you, bro, when I thought about it, I liked it too much.

I think the thing that finally got to Jen up on the tank the other night was when I yelled at her that if we had to, we'd steal her mother's baby and run away. That's still a possibility. I don't want to, though; I hate the idea of starting my Life After High School as a felon with a family. I mean, think of it. There I'd be, going on nineteen, with a baby and a girl friend who can't even be my girl friend, and not clue number one about how to raise a kid. I've read enough— and the shrink out at the college was real clear about this, too—to know that people who have been sexually abused all their lives don't make for the best parents, or partners, right out of the chute, and my guess is Jen has a lot of work to do before she can have a regular life.

But I'll steal that baby before I'll let Jen die. I will, Pres.

What a lot of people don't know—or don't remember—is that I have an ace in the hole. Well, maybe not an ace, but at least a pretty good face card. Okay, maybe it's an eight. Anyway, I'm going to have a choice of citizenships pretty soon. Remember, I was born in Vancouver, B.C., when Mom and Dad were up there for a vacation, so I'm going to have the opportunity to be a Canadian citizen if I want to. If I have to run, that's where I'll go because if I do get caught, they'll have a tougher time getting me back and I can work there if I'm a citizen.

So I've been thinking about all this. I know when things start to move, they'll move fast. I don't want to get caught like I did the other night. If I'd been a second slow in a couple of key spots, I'd be looking through my closet deciding what to wear to Jen's funeral.

But first things first, and now I'm caught in the middle of a lie. I did what I promised I wouldn't: I told. I had to do something, if for no other reason than as I lay there, Jen asleep in my arms, I knew I couldn't keep the responsibility to myself. I decided to tell only one person—either Coach or Dad, but not both. What finally tipped the scales was I figured Coach has probably put up with more bullshit in her life about "inappropriate" sex if she's ruled out marriage, so she'd be the one best able to see that going to the so-called authorities isn't always the smart thing to do. The other thing that helped me make up my mind was that she trapped me. That Coach, she's as smart as ever.

The story we ended up telling her over the phone about Jen's early departure from the game and my looking like I'd been run over by a truck was that Jen had had some kind of chemical imbalance and got so disoriented she just stumbled out into the night. A passing car picked her up and rushed her to the hospital. I got hurt chasing her: slipped on the ice, sprained my ankle, and smashed into a tree, tooth first. Lame. I'll bet you're thinking a guy as smart as I think I am could come up with a better story than that overdosed on Valium.

Coach accepted it over the phone—way too easily, if I'd thought about it; the story had more holes than an octopus's bowling ball—and asked me to come in the next morning and help her with the uniforms, that she'd get the physical therapist from the college to look at my ankle and give me a second opinion.

When I got there, there were no uniforms and no physical therapist. Surprise.

I said, "Aren't teachers supposed to be truthful and

honest, especially when dealing with the fragile psyches of adolescents?" hoping to get in one little bit of humor before it all hit the fan.

"Adolescence has nothing to do with it," Coach said. "I'm honest with people who are honest with me. I wasn't honest with you because I wanted to get you here. I'm about to be honest with you, though, because you're about to be honest with me. What the hell is going on?"

"You're not going to swallow the chemical imbalance theory?"

Coach stared.

"I made it up in virtual isolation," I said. "It sounded good, but I couldn't test it."

Coach stared.

"Jen tried to kill herself."

Coach's expression didn't change. "Tell it all."

So I did. I started with her real dad and then T.B. and told everything I knew: about Jen's fear to leave and her horror at staying; about her fear that her sister is next; and finally about her goddamn pregnant mother. I made sure that at least every fifteen seconds I mentioned the fact that even though people who were supposed to be able to help *knew*, they didn't help.

Coach let me spill my guts, didn't interrupt or ask questions until I was finished.

Then she said, "We have to be very careful what we do next, Dillon. What happens next has to work. You're right. Jen doesn't have many chances left."

God, Pres, it felt like someone lifted a Buick off my shoulders to have Coach with me. I swear this woman is like Allstate. I just burst into tears. I sat there in that chair and cried like a baby. There aren't many people in the world with big enough arms to hold me. I've seen too much and gotten too tough, but Coach moved over to my chair and laid my head against her chest and put her arms around my shoulders—she even shielded my fat lip—and just held me and let me cry, and I thought it would never stop. I had no idea that was all in me. Part of it was you.

When I was done, she moved around to my back and massaged my shoulders while she talked. "We'll go with the chemical imbalance story," she said. "I can fix it up so it sounds a little more likely. I've got to tell the paper something; they've been hounding me all morning. If you see Jen before I do, tell her things are business as usual, that I want to see her an hour before regular dress-down time tonight just to make sure I think she's ready to play. You best spend the day getting that ankle taken care of and working on explaining your missing tooth. Looks nice, by the way, but you might want to see a dentist."

I said, "Thanks, Coach. . . ."

She motioned me toward the door. "Get out of here. Stay with Jen. If *anything* goes wrong I'll be here or at home. Call. If you have to, call 911."

I started to hobble out the door, and Coach offered me a set of crutches that were standing in the corner. "Dillon," she said as I slid them under my arms, "we're against the wall here. I'm breaking the law by not reporting this, and you're taking on an enormous responsibility. There's not a shrink in the world who wouldn't have her hospitalized. We're on instinct here. Don't screw up, okay?"

I said okay. It's a strange thing to be trusted that much by an adult. I'm not sure I like it. If you fall with that responsibility, there's no net.

So things are pretty lively down here. You shouldn't have left so early. We have a couple of plans, so this story could turn downright riveting. Stay tuned.

Dillon

CHAPTER 15

T.B. Martin was a scanner. He could smell trouble at least two steps ahead of the nearest hound dog. That was why, he knew, he was such an effective lawyer: because of his uncanny anticipation of his foe's next move and his uncanny knowledge of the location of his opponent's jugular. If he'd been granted a choice to be any other animal on the planet, he'd have chosen the shark, at least from what he knew of sharks. Sharks never stopped, always on the watch, always looking out. It was that quality in sharks that struck fear in the hearts of humans, and it was that quality in sharks that T.B. respected so.

And there was trouble now. He hadn't been at the game the other night, the one in which his bitch step-daughter had run out, but he talked briefly with her about it and with her mom, and he read the account in the newspaper. He knew damn well no chemical imbalance sent her out into the cold in the middle of an important basketball game. No, something was brewing, and it was about him. He hadn't survived this long and come this far being slow. No way. Mrs. Martin raised no fools.

Women were so stupid! It's a wonder there were enough of them left alive to help propagate the race. You couldn't get a decent response from any of them without the employment of terror, but once you did that, you had them. Look at his wife. For years he had to beat her, had to get into a rage just to deal with her, to stop her infernal clinging and whining. But she was under tow now. Just *knowing* his rage kept her in line. And Jennifer. If it hadn't been for that dog, he might have had more trouble with her, but once he'd crushed his stupid cute little skull into the pavement, well, that was that.

He hadn't spent his childhood locked in closets and tied to his bed doing nothing. He'd thought. In utter darkness he had figured out the world. Even his mother had been a stupid bitch, thinking she would "teach him a lesson once and for all" with her idiotic disciplinary tactics, when all she had really done was make him stronger. And those lightweights she brought home. Fools telling her they could help her get her kid under control. All they had done was prepare him well for life. He was grateful, really, though he'd never let any of them know that. And he didn't have to tell his mom. Good old mom was long gone. Bad car accident. No brakes. How sad.

But something was wrong now, something more immediate. He wasn't too worried. Certainly he had fielded Jennifer's lame attempts at exposing him before, but if she ran out of a *basketball* game, well, at least it needed to be looked at.

Dillon hopped from his bedroom to the top of the stairs when he heard the back door open and close, and his father lay a sack of groceries on the kitchen counter.

"Dad? That you?"

"You know anyone else with a key?" his dad called back. "Of course it's me. How ya doin'? Leg any better?"

"A little," Dillon said, helping himself down the stairs by the banister and hopping across the living room rug to the kitchen door.

"Doc said you were supposed to use the crutches," Caulder said. "Says you slip and bang that thing or step on it accidentally, and you'll likely be crippled up for an extra three weeks." He caught himself. "Hell," he said. "It's your foot."

"It is that," Dillon said. "But you're right. I've been pretty good with it. This is the first time today."

Caulder nodded as he began placing the groceries on the appropriate shelves and in the refrigerator.

"Could we talk about the war?" Dillon asked bluntly.

His father stopped in his tracks but didn't look. "What for?"

"I got this paper," Dillon lied, "and—"

"I thought we had a commitment to truth in this abbreviated family," Caulder said. "Thought we weren't going to bullshit each other."

Dillon grimaced. "What do you mean?"

"I mean, there's been a rule in this house since 1971 that I don't talk about the war. And I have to say I'm pleased it's a rule that's seldom, if ever, been broken. All of a sudden you have a paper, and you want to break a family tradition?" He shook his head. "Tell me why you want to talk about it, then I'll decide."

Dillon took a deep breath. "I want to know about killing."

Caulder was quiet. Finally he said, "They do a lot of it in war."

"I know that. What's it like?"

"Why do you want to know?"

"Because it's important," Dillon said.

Caulder didn't push it. Dillon had always been respectful of his wish to put the Vietnam War behind him, and if he was asking now, there must be a good reason. "It changes a man," Caulder said, and Dillon sat at the table, resting his chin in his hands.

"It changes the way you see the world. You're taught forever that life is sacred, and then it isn't. And it not only isn't *sacred*, it's cheap."

"So how do you justify it?" Dillon asked.

"You don't really," Caulder said. "You just try to stay alive. It's one thing to kill the enemy—to kill someone up there in front of you that's trying to get you before you get him—but in Vietnam we killed when we *weren't sure*. That's where the lines got really blurred." He lowered his head. "If you want to know the truth, that's why I don't talk about the war. I don't know of one infantryman over there who spent any significant time in combat who didn't try to kill someone he wasn't sure about. I did."

"So how do you live with it? I mean, what do you tell yourself?"

"You tell yourself it was war."

"Does that make it okay?"

"It gets you by," Caulder said. "Dillon, they tell you life is sacred, like I said. I've heard that all my life, and I've tried to pass it on. But it isn't, necessarily. It's just life. I think maybe you set the value of your own. By your actions, mostly. You seem to have set yours high; your brother set his low." He smiled. "If I had set mine higher, I wouldn't have gone over there."

"But do you think war justifies killing?"

"Killing can be justified only in the mind of the person doing it," Caulder said. "Justification is a mental process, not a moral imperative." He sat back. "You want to tell me what this is all about?"

Dillon thought a second, then said, "Yeah, I guess I do."

"What're you doing here?" Jennifer asked. "Is something wrong?"

"I don't know," T.B. said. "Thought I might ask you."

The two stood at the sidewalk in front of Chief Joseph High School. It was twelve noon, first lunch break.

"What do you mean?" Jen asked. "You came here to find out if something's wrong?"

"I've been doing a little arithmetic," T.B. said. "And I brought it over here to have you check it for me. You know, see if I made any mistakes."

Jen stared blankly, waiting. She knew better than to play games.

"Why did you run out of the game the other night?"

Jen's heart slipped into overdrive, but she fought it back. "I don't know. I told you, I just got really disoriented."

T.B. nodded. He looked behind her to see a figure approaching on crutches, careful to avoid the icy spots. "Hi, Mr. Martin," Dillon Hemingway said. "What brings you over here?"

"Hi, Dillon. How you doing? Doesn't look like all that well." He nodded toward the crutches.

Dillon smiled. "I've been better. I've been worse. How about Jen, huh? Gonna take us all the way."

"If anyone can, she can," T.B. said, putting an arm on Jen's shoulder.

By now Dillon stood beside them. He'd run out of happy things to say and merely smiled.

"Will you excuse us, Dillon?" T.B. said. "I just need a minute of my daughter's time, and then she's all yours."

"Oh, sure," Dillon said, feigning surprise and

embarrassment for not being more sensitive. "Sure. See you later, huh? Coming to the game Saturday?"

"If I don't have to go out of town." T.B. waved cordially as Dillon worked his way back up the walk toward school, then turned to Jen. "I don't know what that was about the other night, but if you're having any wild ideas about shooting your mouth off again or doing anything foolish or embarrassing, you'd best think twice, young lady."

"I'm not having any wild ideas," Jen said. "I'm not having any ideas at all."

"That's good," he said, tweaking her cheek. "Remember your sister's counting on you."

T.B. turned and waved to Dillon, who stood in the school entrance. "You take care of that leg, you hear?" he yelled. "Won't do to have a trainer who can't take care of himself." He trotted easily to his car, parked in a towaway zone in front of the school. When he had disappeared around the corner, Jen brushed past Dillon and into the girls' bathroom. He tried to follow, but the door closed before he could get to it.

"Talk?" he said fifteen minutes later when she appeared in the doorway, eyes rimmed in red.

Jennifer merely shook her head. "There's nothing to talk about."

"Listen," he said. "Help me out to my van. I've been slipping on these things all day long. Damn maintenance around here isn't worth the powder and fuse."

"Get in," Dillon said at the van. "Let's go for a ride."

"I can't. I've got a class."

"You gonna tell me you stood out there and talked to that creep a half hour ago and now you're gonna get something out of class? Get in."

"Nothing's changed, Dillon," Jennifer said as they drove up Southwest Boulevard away from the school. "No one can touch him. Your doctor friend says I have to be willing to talk. And I am. I *would* talk." Through gritted teeth she said, "But somebody would be dead before I could count to ten. He stopped by the school to warn me about Dawn."

"Then we'll do what we planned," Dillon said. "When the baby's born, we'll steal her and head to Canada, with all signs pointing to California. We'll do whatever we have to do. We'll take Dawn."

"Dillon, what kind of life will we have? We'll be fugitives, for Christ's sake."

"Hey," Dillon said back, "what kind of life do we have now? What kind of life do *you* have?"

Jen was quiet.

"There's one more choice," Dillon said, "if you're willing to let it happen."

"What."

"I could kill him."

Jen snorted. "How are you going to do that? He's one of the best-known lawyers in this town. You gonna challenge him to a duel?"

"Look," Dillon said, and for the first time he let himself consider the possibility seriously. "No one knows I even have a reason to want him dead. I could kill him with Preston's gun and throw it in the river. It's never been registered and no one knows we even have it. The authorities didn't even check for it when Preston killed himself. It's a World War II gun. From Germany. There are probably a hundred of them right here in this town. I could get him clear away from your place. Hell, he's out of town so much I could shoot him in another city."

"Dillon are you out of your mind? You could spend the rest of your life in jail."

"Think about it, Jen. Think about it. See, you're not bothered by the idea of the killing. You're only thinking about the consequences. If I can convince you there won't be any, will you think about it?"

"Of course, killing him wouldn't bother me a bit.

He's killed everyone in my family ten times over. He keeps killing me after I'm dead, and there's an *unborn baby* waiting in line. But I can't let anyone else get hurt in this, Dillon. Especially you. It would kill *me* if something happened to you because of me."

Dillon could see he wouldn't get agreement, but he had the response he needed. He turned around and drove back to school.

CHAPTER 16

Dear Preston,

Well, this may be your last letter from me. I can hear you now. "It's about time! I thought when I got out of high school, I could stop reading forever, and I was *sure* when I killed myself, I could stop reading forever, but leave it to my goddamn semiliterate brother to make me pay beyond the grave." Well, you may get your wish. I've found some people down here who will listen, and for better or worse, things seem to be washing out.

T.B.'s reign is over. An ugly piece of history. I've thought about it a long time, about whether there was anything in me that could feel remorse or sorrow for anything that happened to that man, but there isn't. I'm sorry his life was whatever it was to allow him to turn out like he did, but I can't be sorry for *him*.

I finally figured out that all of the legitimate avenues to put an end to what was happening to Jen were blocked. If it had been just a question of her making enough noise to get the child protection authorities involved, I think she would have done it, even though she'd failed before. That Dr. Newcomb guy out at the college carries some weight and he would have backed Jen all the way. In fact, when she finally went out there with me to talk to him, she was even a little bit encouraged. But the bottom line was that it all would have taken too much time, and her stepdad had upped the ante so high we just didn't have it. I mean, this guy struck like lightning. He knew something was up, that Jen was about to crack one way or the other, and you know what he told her? Jeezuz. He told her that he had never expected to last this long with her family, that he'd expected to have had to take *drastic measures* long before this, and that it was a testament to her sense of discretion that everyone was alive and well. He told her he could disappear in a heartbeat if he had to and show up within three months on the East Coast with a full-blown successful family law practice. I don't know whether he could honestly pull that off, or whether he really had destroyed other families before he came into Jen's life, like he said he had, but she sure believed him. And if I had to bet a month's pay one way or the other, I sure wouldn't bet against him. You should have seen this guy, Pres. He followed no rules. None.

He's following one now, though.

I thought of all the ways, Pres. I even further developed the plan to help Jen steal her mother's baby when it's born and head up across the border. I was going to become a Canadian Ironman. Actually, I was going to become a Canadian Familyman.

But I gotta tell you about Dad. God, Pres, we didn't know him. I'll always be proud to be the son of a man who can carry so much *weight* with so much dignity, even though I know it's not good for his insides. He's pretty sure that's one of the reasons Mom left, when you were crippled and on drugs and headed on your crash course with gravity and she couldn't get him to talk. But he can sure make that Gary Cooper act look good. And he's got real integrity. I've waited a long time to use that word well, and I can use it now for Dad.

I swore I wasn't going to tell a bunch of people about Jen because I didn't want anyone going off to do the "right thing" and getting somebody hurt or killed. So I chose Coach because she always seems so level-headed, and like I said, I even got Jen to go see Dr. Newcomb with me as long as she didn't have to use her name. But none of that made a difference because Jen was too spooked to take any action. Then one night I was talking with Dad, broke the lifelong family edict banning discussions of the war, and I realized he was the one to tell all along. If anyone can make me understand things, it's Dad. And I know he'd go to the wall. I think I didn't know that before because I didn't ask.

He listened to my story, didn't spend a second trying to pick it apart or get me to "go through the proper channels" or any of that bullshit I already knew wouldn't work. When he'd heard it all, he asked me what I planned to do.

I said, "I'm not sure, Dad. I might have to kill him."

That shocked him some, I think, because he could tell I was serious, but he didn't show a lot of alarm. He showed common sense. He said, "You should think real carefully about that, Dillon. What you're talking about will only add to the tragedy."

I said that it was the only thing I could think of and that I couldn't just stand by and watch anymore.

He said, "How do you think your friend will feel if she has to add one more ruined life to her list, from what you tell me, probably the only life apart from her sister's that she really cares about?"

That was close to what I needed to hear, that I'd be causing as much pain as I'd be relieving—Dad really knows me—but I wasn't convinced there was any other way. He was careful. He didn't challenge my ability to try something really stupid. He said, "It's not a question of whether or not you could pull it off, Dillon, it's whether you'd do more damage than good to yourself or the person you're trying to help." Then he asked me not to make any crazy plans without talking to him again.

I got up to leave, and when I got to the door, he said, "Dillon," and I turned around. "If you killed him, he'd just be *dead*. Is that enough?"

That's what changed my mind. Dad didn't appeal to my sense of reason or count on the off chance that I might come to my senses and actually project on what the taking of a life might mean to me later on or what my life in prison might be like. No way. He appealed to my sense of revenge because he knew it was the only sense available. Our daddy's a three-point shooter, Pres. He has *touch*.

If I had thought about all the possible consequences of what I did next, I might not have done it, but I think it's a blessing—or a curse—of adolescence not to place a whole lot of value on the idea of thought before action. I knew I needed to show T.B. up close and personal, as they say, without including Jen in on the agony of his defeat. That's not something that can be done aboveboard, when there are as many limitations as were placed on me in this situation, so I took a chapter right out of T.B.'s own life. I figured he's gotten away with this crap for so long because of the element of unbelievability; no one can *imagine* a regular, married, employed human being capable of such acts. They just can't picture it. So I decided to do something so off the wall no one would possibly see it coming until it had already went. I got Coach to get me back in contact with Wayne Wisnett, the news guy she goes out with. I don't know whether you remember or not, but I did a research paper at the beginning of my sophomore year on those neo-Nazis that live over in Hayden Lake, in north Idaho. Well, this Wisnett was the guy who did the undercover news report on those unconscious bootlicks, and he had helped me out with some of the details for my paper. And I knew he liked me because he did a little feature when I won my age division in my first triathlon about a year later. He told Coach he thought I was "unique." Anyway, I remembered that when he infiltrated those jerks over in Hayden, he gathered all his visual evidence with a small video camera that uses infrared light or some such hi-tech "Star Wars" bullshit and *takes pictures in the dark.* It wasn't easy to convince him and I might have had help from voices in the universe; but for whatever reason, old Wayne took a flyer on me, checked that zillion-dollar piece of machinery out to himself without making me tell him what I was going to do with it and even gave me lessons on how to make it work and how to set the timer, though there's really not much to it. He did all that right before he told me which tree I'd find my butt nailed to if it had so much as a scratch on it.

Things get a little strange with this story from here, and I still don't know how I feel about having done what I did, but when I picked up Jen and her sister to go over to the second game of the regional basketball tournament, they let me inside because their parents were gone. I used the upstairs bathroom and on my way back got a peek at Jen's room, where I scouted out the best spots to plant that little hummer. The reason things get strange is that I knew if Jen had an inkling what I was planning, she would have crammed a banana down my throat, then reached down in there to peel it. I didn't think I'd ever tell her, really, but I had to figure the odds of her finding out on her own were at least fifty-fifty. But desperate times call for desperate measures, as they say. And I guess they call for desperate people, too, 'cause I was feeling *all* of that. Anyway, the next night when I picked them up to go to the final game, I put a piece of one of Dad's old plastic credit cards in the latch on the way out so it wouldn't lock, and along about the second quarter of the game I got violently ill and had to leave. I hauled ass back over to Jen's place and let myself in. Now I ain't a religious man—you know that, Pres—but I could be persuaded to believe that God was one of the architects of that bedroom because right above the closet, out of anyone's reach, there was this absolutely useless bookshelf with a piece of drapery hanging over it that somebody must have put there to hide it from view. I rested a little easier when I found about three inches of dust on the surface. Anyway, I propped the camera with a couple of paperback books and parted the curtain just a *hair* so it stared right down on Jen's bed, and I set the timer for the next night, when I knew El Creepo would be home.

I didn't really think I'd get it on the first try, but when I saw Jen in English class, she looked like death taking a crap, and I was pretty sure I'd scored.

It was a hell of a lot more trouble getting that thing out of there than it was planting it. Jen almost never let me in the house when her parents were home, and it took me *three* goddamn days to get to it. Every night when I went to bed, I was *sure* the phone would ring and we'd get the news that the whole family had been wiped out, and that's the only time I really wished I hadn't done it. I was so crazy paranoid by the time I finally got back in there I thought I was going to just drop in my tracks of cardiac surprise.

But when I got back over there, excusing myself to the upstairs bathroom within seconds of walking through the door, I got into Jen's room and peeled back that curtain, and there that little jewel sat, big old smile on its lens saying, "Have a nice day," having added a full-length feature of the escapades of one psychopathic sexual pervert to its list of dubious visual chronicles.

I'm sorry, Pres. I have to use the sarcasm because if I don't, I can't write this without throwing up. Until that day the hardest thing I ever went through was watching you kill yourself. But sitting there in my dark room after I got back home, more goddamn alone than I've ever been in my life, and so scared I couldn't keep my insides out of my throat, watching that vicious asshole utterly violate this person I cared so much about, well, it bumped you down to second place. I wanted to run. I wanted to run so fast and far that I'd drop, but I couldn't get to the end of the icy walk on these damned crutches, so I buried my face in my pillow and screamed and screamed until my throat bled. I don't know how I got through the night, Pres. I don't. I thought finally things had gotten so downright ugly that you were right: that there was only one way out of all this. But I hung in there. I did. At one point I started to go to sleep, but that tape was rewound in my head, just waiting for me to dare close my eyes. Finally I turned on all the lights and sat up in the bed and stared at the wall and hummed Gene Autry and Roy Rogers tunes off those old 45 rpm records Mom and Dad gave us when you turned six, and I waited for the sun to come up. I didn't think it ever would; I really thought the world had turned into one long, unbearable night, but finally I could see the silhouette of the garage roof out my window, and pretty soon the yard was bathed in the same soft orange of the morning of your last day, and I knew I had made it.

I thought I could wait for Dad to leave and hook his VCR up to mine to make the copies I needed, but the tape in those fancy little spy gizmos isn't the same as they use, and I had to get Wayne to make them for me. Man, I owe that guy. I just came right out and begged him not to watch while he made them, and he let me stay right there in the room to see that he didn't. I don't know if he took one look at me and knew how close to the edge I was or if he was just so glad to get his camera back in one piece that he'd have done anything I asked, but I owe him big. He just made the copies, gave them to me—wouldn't even take money—and sent me on my way. All he said was "I hope this is all worth it, Ironman. You look like hell."

I took his concern under advisement and went back to work out my delivery system—should something unexpected happen to me—and to shower, shave, and freshen my handsome self up a bit so I could go downtown and make some arrangements for a safe-deposit box before I went to have a little chat with a scumball lawyer. Didn't wear a tie, but I dragged out the leather sports jacket. I'd have worn slacks, dealing in the business world and all, but none of mine fit over the cast, so I cut the seam in the leg of a new pair of Levi's and wore those. You'd have been proud, bro. On the inside I was definitely crazed, but on the outside I looked cool and calm. (In one of the conversations I'd had with Dr. Newcomb—a conversation I remembered *very* well—he'd said, "There's a cliche in this business, Dillon. You can't lie to children or psychopaths. It's not completely true, though. Fact is, you can lie to children. But if you ever have reason to take this guy on—and I suggest you don't—have your bases covered. Never try to bluff him. He's a dangerous man.") So I took the elevator in the Brooks Building up to the top floor and walked into the Martin, Lofler & Williams law firm like I knew what the hell I was doing. It was about ten minutes to noon, and I caught old T.B. headed out all by himself for a two-martini lunch gathering of Perverts Unanimous.

He looked a little startled to see me, and I walked right up to him and asked if I could have a few minutes of his time, and he was cordial like he always is but said he was real busy right now and could I come back later. I said, "Nope."

He looked at the tape case in my hand and back in my eyes, and I was scared as hell; but I held the tape up and said, "I have something you should see."

So we went in, and I asked if he had something we could

take a look at the tape on, and he called to his secretary, and she whipped right in and set it up.

I almost stopped right there, Pres. I almost stopped because I couldn't imagine watching it again, and I was really afraid what would happen if he saw my reaction—like he'd think he had me—but then I remembered how Jen told me that when he came into her room at night, she just went away. I figured if it was good enough for her, it was good enough for me. So old T.B. Martin, that pillar of our community, that president-elect of FUTURE THREE FORKS, slid the tape right into his thousand-dollar machine, cranked up his twenty-seven-inch stereo Sony TV set, and he and I watched us some serious video.

I took his pulse from the veins in his forehead and said, "This is your copy. I have several more."

He watched awhile and took a deep breath, straightened his tie. Then he smiled and said, "What do you want?"

I said, "I want you gone."

He said, "I'm afraid that's not possible."

I nodded toward the video. "This shit's gonna be pretty hard to explain."

He put a finger up to his lip and watched some more, nodding, measured me, then glanced over to his desk.

"You could do that," I said, fantasizing a gun in the top middle drawer, "but anything happens to me and one copy goes to each of the TV channels, one to the newspaper, one to the cops, and one to the prosecutor's office. I took the time to write a clear narrative. You have to know I wouldn't be here if I weren't covered. And you must know I *know* what you're like, or I'd be at the police station. There's no bluff. I'm not stupid."

He nodded again. "And if I go along?"

"I leave the tapes where they are."

He said, "What do I have to do to get them?"

I said, "Die."

"How do I know you won't make them public?"

"I wouldn't do that to Jen. She knows nothing about this. She's suffered enough; I won't add to that unless I have to. I hate you a lot, but I love her more. But if anything happens, like to a family pet, you asshole, or to her sister or her or her mom, and I mean *anything*, these things will be prime time."

He stared straight ahead, seemingly scanning the possibilities, and my stomach rolled. What if I'd left some hole open? What if I'd missed just one little piece? "Accidents count," I said.

"What?"

"Accidents," I said. "They count. If someone in Jen's family has an accident, or if I do, or if her little sister's pet gerbil does, that counts. Tapes hit the mail trail."

"That's not something I can control."

"Then you better hope you're lucky."

Then I saw just a *little* crack, a tic at the corner of his mouth. He said, "You know, you little faggot, I could beat this in court. You may not know who you're dealing with."

I shrugged. "Be my guest. I've got good people behind me if I need them. Not public defenders with caseloads backed up into the alley. Good people. Smart ones. Some maybe as smart as you."

He thought another minute and took a deep breath, again unflappable. "How long?" he asked. "How long will you give me to get things squared away."

"Five, maybe ten minutes," I said. "When we walk out of here, you go home and get your shit, leave a note that says you have to go out of town for a week, and you're gone. Communication with these people is over. Jen said once that you told her you could be set up three thousand miles away in three months. That sounds like a distance I could tolerate."

The son of a bitch wouldn't let me see him sweat, Pres. He's hard core. *Really* hard core. He just nodded and said, "You got me."

I followed him to his house, and he packed a suitcase and took some boxes of things, and at the car I told him, "It's automatic. Anything happens to anyone remotely involved in this, and the VCR express opens its gates."

He said, "I said you got me. Okay?"

I said, "We'll see."

I thought that would do it, Pres. I thought I had covered all my bases and now he'd just disappear and no one would know what happened to him and life could go on like it was designed to do. But it was too easy. I went to bed that night thinking what a genius I'd turned out to be, and by the time I'd lain in the dark for about thirty minutes I was in complete and utter panic. He was just too smart and too mean to go out without a whimper. I didn't know for sure what I'd missed; but I knew it had to be something major, and I had probably assured my part as an accessory in a family bloodbath. So I went down and woke up Dad and told him.

He listened, and after he passed through pure astonishment, he said, "I tell you, son, I don't know enough about that kind of man to give you any help at all. Sounds like you covered all the bases to me, but who knows?" He decided the man who did know would be Dr. Newcomb, so we gave him a call at his home, and next thing I knew Dad was driving us out there.

The good doctor said it was entirely possible that he was gone, but that I'd been crazy to try to take a guy like

T.B. Martin on alone. He said, "If there's a hole, he'll find it. I think you need to warn his family."

Well, hell, by then it was nearly midnight, but Dad drove me back home to get your van—I didn't want Jen to know anyone else knew—and I went over there and banged on the door until a light came on upstairs, and pretty soon Jen answered.

I thought she would rip my head off. She screamed at me and hammered on my chest and actually knocked me down into the snow. No one has ever said as vicious things as that to me—ever. She told me that I'd betrayed her and I was like everyone else in her life and that she could see why you'd want to kill yourself because of me and that she hoped every day of my life from now on would feel just exactly like it did the minute you pulled the trigger. And she said that she hated my guts and that I would rot in hell.

I couldn't understand it, Pres, I just couldn't. But then it got crystal clear. Jen knelt beside my head in the snow—I'd been afraid to get up—and she grabbed my face in her hands and she said, "Do you know the one thing in the world worse than having that bastard on me all the time? Inside me?" and all I could do was shake my head no, and she said, "It's having someone *watch* it. It's having someone see it. And *know* it. Do you understand that?" Do you understand that?" and she shoved my head back into the snow and stomped into the house. I lay there in the snow, stunned, and I did understand. Not in the way Jen knew it, but in the best way I could without having gone through it, I think.

When she went back inside, I pulled myself up and dug around in the snow for my crutches, made it to my car, and drove off; but I came back and parked on the other side of the street, where I could see both the front and back of her house, so I could be sure she wouldn't head out for a bridge or a water tower or some damn thing. God, I felt awful.

It was a week before she would even acknowledge my existence. She wouldn't let me touch her all during the state tournament, even to wrap her leg. I finally had to tell Coach about it, and she took care of Jen's training needs. On the night of the state final over in Seattle—we won it, by the way, in the anticlimactic event of the decade—she touched me on the arm. Didn't say anything, mind you, but she touched my arm.

Who knows what her mind went through in that time, but on the bus ride back, she came over and asked the girl sitting next to me to move, and she sat down and said, "Do you have the copies of those tapes?"

I said I did.

She said, "Can I have them?"

I told her of course she could have them.

"I'm taking them to the police." Pres, I'll tell you, sometimes I think this whole part of my life was orchestrated by some amateur spirit rehearsing to be a minor god in charge of keeping people off-balance. I said, "What?"

Jen said, "If T.B.'s out there somewhere, then it won't be long before some girl is in the same boat as I've been in. I don't know who she is, but I can't let that happen to anyone if I have a chance to stop it. I talked to that Dr. Newcomb guy long distance on the phone this morning before we left, and he said he could help me with the legal part. He said he could probably see to it that I never have to watch the tape."

I looked into her eyes. "What if you do?"

She grimaced. "Then I do."

We rode along in silence for a while. Then she said, "I'm still mad at you, Dillon. But at least I know why you did it."

I still don't know how all this will turn out. Jen went to the police and the prosecutor with Dr. Newcomb, and he's going to do some therapy with her. They promised to run the investigation without any publicity, and unless T.B.

turns up, Jen won't have to worry.

Jen and Stacy have become good friends; they spend an incredible amount of time together. Jen is totally transfixed by Ryan, and sometimes I think the little mucous factory has two mothers. Two eighteen-year-olds. Does that make one thirty-six? I'm pretty sure Jen told Stacy all about her stepdad; they're really tight now, and I don't think you can become that close without sharing the tough stuff. Part of me is jealous, I mean—you should *see* them together—but another part is relieved. It's kind of nice not being the one who knows all and can't tell.

I've backed way off anything romantic. I ain't the smartest guy in the world, but I'm smart enough to know what Dr. Newcomb said about Jen has to be true, and it's going to be a long time before she's ready to be with anyone, and even if she did get better, I have this deep feeling—so deep it's almost like *knowledge*—that she wouldn't even be able to be with me, me having seen that tape and all.

But whatever Jen is or isn't, she's one hell of a round-baller. I swear, the harder things got for her in the world, the tougher she was on the court. I want to tell you she tore them *up* at state. If this all ever settles down, I think she'll be real proud.

It looks like Jen's mom will give her baby up for

adoption. The day after she found out what I'd done, Jen went right to her and said that she was going to tell everything if her mom didn't give it up, that she didn't have idea number one how to protect it and Jen was living proof of that, and that she was by God going to see it didn't go one step farther. It's amazing to me that the only way to get anything done in that family is through blackmail. I guess Mrs. Martin cried and begged for another chance, but Jen laid down her ultimatum and walked out of the room.

You'd like my new tooth, the one I got to replace the hole Jen left in my face. I found this bizarre dentist with a sense of humor that matches mine pretty closely, and for a few extra bucks—actually a *lot* of extra bucks—he puts metallic and ceramic inlays into his bridgework. Now I have a gold star right in the middle of my front tooth, and every time he sees me smile, Caldwell nearly craps his drawers with indignation. I guess he doesn't remember Gus Johnson of the old Baltimore Bullets in the NBA. I'm saving my money for a ceramic inlay of the Tasmanian Devil.

Well, bro, I guess that about wraps it. No more homework for you. I've got better things to do with my life than spend it with a pen in my hand, writing to a man who never reads his mail. My struggle with you is finished. I'm going to let you go, push my finger in and release us from these crazy Chinese handcuffs.

I wish you'd stayed, though.

God, how I wish you'd stayed.

Your brother,

Dillon

EPILOGUE

Dillon stood in Coach Sherman's office, folding the girls' uniforms for the final time, his stint as trainer for the State Champion Chief Joseph Braves officially at an end.

"Do I get a girls' letter jacket?" he asked.

"Do you want one?"

"Sure. The managers and trainers of all the boys' sports get them."

"It's okay with me," Coach said. "You can fill out one of those order forms on the desk."

Dillon smiled. "I think it will be a spiritual challenge for Caldwell to see me in a girls' letter jacket with a gold star in my smile every day from now till the end of school." He seemed to consider something a minute, then: "Coach, can I ask you a question?"

"Sure."

"What's it feel like knowing you're always going to be alone?"

Coach smiled. "I guess it's like being free. Being alone isn't bad at all when it's a choice."

"But what's it *like*?"

She put down the shorts she was folding and sat against the desk. "It's like being tall, or blond, or quick. It's just what I am. It's what is."

Dillon squinted and grimaced a little, obviously hoping for something more revealing.

"Dillon, the so-called American Dream isn't for everyone. It's particularly not for a lot of women. See, we get to be dreamed about, but we don't often get to do the dreaming. We become part of the collection of artifacts that make up that dream for men. At its worst, it turns into what happened in Jen's family. Some women can pull it off, some even pull it off well, but it's a standard to measure against, rather than one to aspire to." She smiled. "Because I live by myself doesn't mean I'm alone. It just means I have the choice. And I like that."

Dillon nodded.

Coach said, "Are you worried about being alone?"

He smiled. "A little, I guess."

"Just remember it's a choice. Like everything else, it's a choice."

Dillon drove his brother's van through town toward his old neighborhood, where he and Preston had grown up together, across the back alley from Mrs. Crummet, and Charlie the Cat. He pulled into the alley and parked up close to the side of the old garage, next to a box of rusty car parts, placed there years ago to mark the site of a savage killing. He got out of the van and stood staring at the box, wondering if his memory of the events on that long-ago summer evening connected him in any way to T.B. Martin. He imagined it did.

He crossed the alley, approached the back porch, then knocked lightly on the screen door. When no one answered, he rang the bell, and a small, pretty woman, probably in her mid-thirties, appeared. "Yes?"

"Hi," he said. "My name is Dillon Hemingway, and I used to live in that house next door. There was an old woman living here then. Her name was Mrs. Crummet. Do you by any chance know what happened to her?"

"Sure," the woman said, opening the screen door. "She lives right here with us." She put out her hand. "I'm Betty. She's my mother."

Dillon nodded and smiled. "Do you suppose I could see her?"

The woman motioned him in. "Certainly," she said. "She'd love to see you, I'm sure. To tell you the truth, she doesn't get many visitors."

The woman led Dillon into the living room, where an ancient lady sat rocking in her chair. She didn't look up as they entered the room, and the woman walked directly in front of her, bent down, and raised her voice gently. "Mom," she said, "this is Dillon Hemingway. He used to live next door. He came to see you."

Mrs. Crummet looked around the room, seemingly startled when her eyes came to rest on Dillon, who stood before her, his hands folded in front of him. "Hi, Mrs. Crummet. Do you remember me?"

Mrs. Crummet stared back as if she hadn't the foggiest notion who this boy was. Her daughter stood and whispered in his ear, "She gets confused, Dillon. She's pretty old. Eighty-three last month."

Dillon knelt down to her eye level. "I used to live next door," he said, and Mrs. Crummet nodded, still without any recognition whatever. "Hemingway," he said.

Mrs. Crummet said, "Hemingway," then started

with recognition. "You used to live next door," she said. "Daddy's a mailman or a truck driver or something."

"Yeah," Dillon said. "That's me. Do you remember a cat you used to have? A cat named Charlie?"

"Charlie," Mrs. Crummet said with a faraway look. "Charlie. Oh, yes. Charlie. He's out back. In the wood-pile."

"No," Dillon said. "This was a three-legged cat you had about ten years ago. He disappeared."

"Three legs?" she said. "Oh, yes. Three legs. Had to chop one of 'em off. It was just hanging there. Charlie. Yes. He's out back in the woodpile."

Dillon closed his eyes. "He's not out there, Mrs. Crummet. My brother and I—we killed him."

"Well, you boys should be ashamed," she said. "The very idea. . . . What were you doing out there?"

"No," Dillon said. "I mean, it was ten years ago. We killed Charlie. It was stupid. He hurt our dog."

"He hurt your dog?" Mrs. Crummet was indignant. "I'll have a word with Charlie this afternoon. Is your dog all right?"

"Our dog's fine," Dillon said. "I mean, he's old now. He's gone. But I came to tell you about your cat. I came to say I'm sorry."

Mrs. Crummet's eyes went soft and faraway. "Well,

that's nice," she said. "More people should say that. More people should say they're sorry."

Tears welled in Dillon's eyes. He ran his fingers softly over her wrist, and she placed her other hand over them as he stared into her face and she gazed out beyond the kitchen doorway, across the alley to an old box full of rusty car parts.

Her daughter put a hand on Dillon's shoulder. "She doesn't understand," she said. "I do, though. Let yourself off the hook, Dillon. You were a little boy."

He stood, staring sadly at Mrs. Crummet before her daughter walked him back toward the kitchen door, where he thanked her and said, "I guess some things just can't be fixed."

In late summer a police detective in Orlando, Florida, walked into a plush law office in a tall office building only a few minutes' drive from Disney World. Without identifying himself he approached a handsome, tanned middle-aged lawyer standing in the waiting room, talking with his secretary. "Are you Terrence Martin?" he asked.

"Why, yes, I am," T.B. said, extending his hand.

"I have a warrant for your arrest," the detective said. "You have the right to remain silent . . ."

Three days later Dillon Hemingway entered his first triathlon in more than a year and placed third in his age-group, eighteenth overall, with a time more than twenty minutes faster than he'd projected.

His former high school principal, John Caldwell, was heard to say, "What a waste. It's a real shame I could never teach that kid any respect."

More great books

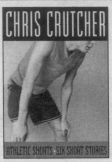

ATHLETIC SHORTS: SIX SHORT STORIES

Hc 0-688-10816-4
Pb 0-06-050783-7

These six stories include characters from some of Crutcher's best-loved novels, as well as unforgettable new personalities, in tales of love, death, bigotry, heroism, and coming of age.

IRONMAN

Hc 0-688-13503-X
Pb 0-06-059840-9

Dangerously close to expulsion from school, triathlete Bo Brewster is assigned to an Anger Management class, where he addresses his difficult relationship with his father.

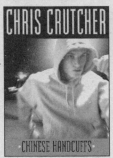

CHINESE HANDCUFFS

Hc 0-688-08345-5
Pb 0-06-059839-5

Two star athletes, Dillon and Jennifer, find the courage to confront painful memories in this gritty, realistic tale of friendship and healing.

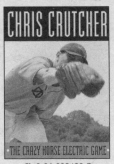

THE CRAZY HORSE ELECTRIC GAME

Pb 0-06-009490-7

A freak accident robs Will of his once-amazing physical talents. He must fight his way back in a San Francisco school for troubled youth.

www.harperteen.com   www.chriscrutcher.com

HarperCollins*Children'sBooks*

from Chris Crutcher!

Hc 0-688-02002-X
Pb 0-06-009491-5

A young athlete stands up for his beliefs and quits the team, then falls apart when his girlfriend dies.

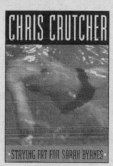

Hc 0-688-11552-7
Pb 0-06-009489-3

Sarah Byrnes and Eric Calhoune have been friends since junior high. Now Sarah sits silent in a hospital. Can Eric uncover her terrible secret before it puts them both in danger?

Hc 0-688-05715-2
Pb 0-06-009492-3

Four friends push themselves to their physical limits, and learn one another's deepest secrets.

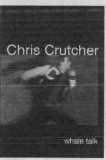

Hc 0-688-18019-1

T. J. Jones brings together a band of misfits to carve their own space as the swim team at a school that has no pool.